CAMP SILVER OAKS

BY LEEROY CROSS JAMES

To request permissions, contact the publisher at
leeroycrossjames@hotmail.com.

Edited by David-Jack Fletcher - **Chainsaw Editing.**
Cover by Donnie Goodman - **Atonic Vision Design.**

ISBN: 9798840358689

CW: This book contains violence, scenes of a sexual nature and gore.

JUST LIKE BART, I LOVE A PLAYLIST.
WANT TO LISTEN TO THE TUBULAR TUNES
THAT ARE FEATURED IN THE BOOK AND
HELPED INSPIRE CAMP SILVER OAKS?
SCAN THE QR CODE BELOW!

CAMP SILVER OAKS: THE SOUNDTRACK

OR HEAD ON OVER TO SPOTIFY AND
SEARCH FOR CAMP SILVER OAKS: THE
SOUNDTRACK.

CONTENTS

"YOU'RE GOING TO CAMP BLOOD, AIN'T
YA?
IT'S GOT A DEATH CURSE!"

CRAZY RALPH — FRIDAY THE 13TH, 1980.

PROLOGUE

CAMP STANLEYSIDE
1980

The sun had been blaring all day. Even as the night began to draw in, casting shadows from the trees like long crooked fingers stretching across the cabins, the heat was close to being unbearable. So much so that Charley Reiner couldn't sit in the mess hall for much longer. The stench of that night's dinner—sloppy joes—was bad enough, but the sickening sweet odor of hormonal teenagers? Too gross.

Haven't any of these kids heard of soap and water? he thought, attempting to breathe through his mouth and swallow the soggy, saturated bun from the sloppy joe at the same time. It made him gag and a lump of saliva—thick with the stale scent of teenagers—went down his throat.

The other counselors at the table tucked into their meals without a word between them, almost like the smell didn't exist. Like it was all in Charley's head. Together, they looked like an unusual bunch. Coming from different towns, all having different interests. It showed by their dress sense. Carla still thought the flower power movement was in full force, judging by the floral headband she always wore, and Eric looked like the long-lost brother from Bee Gees. Charley hated the Bee Gees. But they all got along just fine. Melissa—a cheerleader from Blackhill—grinned at Charley halfway through chewing her sloppy joe. The gooey mess stuck to her teeth, and she looked as though she'd been chewing on shit. The brown goo matched her eyes. Charley smiled back and shifted his plate to the middle of the table.

Satisfied that she had his attention, Melissa swooped the length of her poker-straight red hair over one shoulder and fanned at her sweat-glistened neck. Sure, she was obvious. Charley knew the signals, he'd been getting them from her and Tawny—another counselor from Blackhill—since the season started. It was nothing new. Girls always seemed to flirt with him, though he had no idea why. He inherited his dad's crooked teeth, Mom's bushy eyebrows, and he was under no illusion that he would bald prematurely. All the other men in his family did. It didn't help that he noticed more and more hair in the shower plug every day. So, he didn't see what the fuss was all about. Of course, that didn't mean he wouldn't take the opportunity to soak up the attention while he still could.

You're only young once, right?

"I'm gonna go for a walk," Charley said, no longer able to stand the heat, the food, or the smell of body odor. "You guys okay to deal with the kids?"

They all nodded. Melissa batted her eyes at him as she did so, but Charley pretended not to notice.

The temperature wasn't much better outside, but at least the camp smelled like fresh pines. Charley strolled through the path where the cabins sat in uneven rows either side of him. He studied them as he walked past, proud of the paint job he did on the wood before the kids had arrived a few weeks before. At first, he wasn't sure about taking the job at Camp Stanleyside, mainly because he hated kids, but overall, he enjoyed the job so far. It beat working in some stuffy store all summer or baking every day indoors. At least he had the fresh air, the use of the lake and plenty of time to play baseball. His personal passion.

Just as he was about to go inside his cabin, he stopped in his tracks. One of the kids was sitting on the grass outside, weaving a small snake between his fingers.

"AJ! Put that down!" Charley said, backing away. Trying not to show how much he was freaked out by the vile little serpent-devil. "You should be in the mess hall—haven't you had any dinner yet?"

"Not hungry," the kid mumbled without taking his eyes away from the slippery creature slithering between his knuckles.

Charley took a deep breath to prepare himself. He stormed over and grabbed AJ's hand, shaking the snake onto the grass, and dragging the kid by his wrist. "I don't care if you're hungry or not. You know the rules."

Like the brat he was, AJ attempted to bolt from Charley so he could get the snake before it got away, but Charley tightened his grip. "No! Let me play with him! He's my friend!"

"Here's an idea, why don't you go and play with someone you can actually talk to?"

AJ scowled at his counselor. He tried to push Charley away, but it was no use. Charley was nearly three times his size. "They all think I'm weird…"

Finally, Charley loosened his grip. Once he let go, AJ fell flat on his ass and screwed up his face, about to burst into tears. "Well, I wonder why when you're talking to snakes of all things."

With tight balled fists, AJ wiped at his eyes so hard they left red rings around the sockets. "I hate you…" he hissed.

"Oh, you break my heart," Charley said, pouting, and placed

a hand on his chest. "Now fuck off!"

AJ picked himself up from the ground, frantically looking around in the grass for his pet, scared to put his foot in the wrong place in case he squashed the little monster.

"Forget the snake," Charley said, taking a step back and looking at the grass around his feet. "If I ever see that thing again, I'll stomp on it myself. Do you understand?"

It was clear by the mix of hatred and fear in the kid's eyes that he got the message, and it was enough to make him finally do as he was told. Charley watched as AJ ran down the path, back to the mess hall. He shook his head as he watched the kid run.

"How much do I get paid for this crap again?" he mumbled. Still, it was worth it for the baseball and the lake.

As soon as he was inside his cabin, Charley whipped off his sweaty shirt and went to his drawer to choose the evening's clothes. Shorts, tube socks, a fresh pair of briefs. He rummaged around for a clean shirt and picked out a yellow crop top.

"Perfect!"

While the kids were eating, he'd have the shower block to himself. At least the water would be hot. He threw the clothes on his bed and went to grab his wash bag from the bedside table when he noticed a piece of lined paper sitting on his pillow. It was folded in half.

Charley snatched the piece of paper and grinned when he read the message.

MEET ME BY THE LAKE AFTER THE SOCIAL

M x

*

Charley snuck out of the mess hall while the social was still underway. The kids and the counselors were just getting into Blondie's *Call Me*, dry humping each other all over the place, so nobody would notice him slipping out. The night was as hot as the day—if not hotter—and it was sticky. At least he was clean and smelled fresh, though. He even blow-dried his hair for the occasion. Not that it did much good in the humidity or the dark, but it was always good to make an impression when you were about to get your rocks off.

Debbie Harry's vocals faded as Charley trotted down the path toward the lake. Stepping closer to the water, he welcomed the cool breeze. In the dark he saw the black silhouette of his date for the night, resting against the steps that led up to the dock. He stopped to place a hand down the waistband of his shorts. The excitement had already got to him and pressed awkwardly against his briefs. Once he adjusted his dick and balls, he was good to go and jogged the rest of the way down to the dock.

"A note again, seriously?" Charley said. "Not exactly 'discreet', is it?"

Out of the darkness, the figure swayed slowly toward him, brushing back blonde curls, and wearing a tight polo with denim cut-offs. "Well, I was careful. I didn't write 'Mike' this time."

Charley smiled and leaned in closer, resting both of his arms over Mike's strong shoulders. "You look hot," he said, before planting a kiss on his lips.

Mike responded by placing his hands on Charley's waist and pushed it toward his own so they could enjoy a longer kiss.

The excitement had got to Mike, too.

"Come on," he said, grabbing Charley's hand, "we don't have long."

Charley cocked an eyebrow. "It won't take me long."

"That's not something to brag about, dude."

Doing as he was told for a change, Charley allowed Mike to guide him to the woods near the lake. Before they entered, something—a twig maybe—snapped.

Charley pulled away from Mike's hand. "Wait," he said. "Did you hear that?"

Mike shook his head. "No. What?"

"I heard something."

"Come on." Mike sighed, grabbing Charley's hand once again.

There was a moment of hesitance when Mike tried to pull him forward, but Charley finally gave in, and they entered the woods.

Even with the moonlight breaking through the gaps between the trees, it was hard to see where they were going. Although it hadn't rained for days, the ground was soggy and wet under his sneakers. Charley began to worry about getting them muddy. The other counselors wouldn't question it even if he was covered in dirt, they weren't neat freaks like he was. It was the burden of having to clean them that he was more concerned about. He saved up months of his allowance to buy them.

Once they were far away enough from the camp, Mike positioned Charley against a tree so he could rest his back on the trunk. They continued to make-out while Mike undid the drawstring of Charley's shorts and tugged them down.

There better not be any squirrel shit on the ground, he thought, struggling to get into the mood.

Even as Mike kissed his neck and carried on all the way

down to his stomach, it was like he was numb to his touch. Charley was a big boy, he wasn't afraid of the dark. Not usually. But something felt *off* about tonight. He put it down to the paranoia of getting caught and tried to shake the jitters away so he could enjoy the moment. He finally started to relax and pressed his hand into Mike's messy curls. Then just as he closed his eyes…

SNAP.

"What was that?" Charley's first instinct was to push Mike's head away from his crotch.

Sighing, Mike made his way back up from the ground, dusting himself off. "I don't know, it's probably just a bird or something—did you really have to push me away like that? Jesus…"

The woods were completely silent now. All Charley could hear was their short breaths. Mike stood with his hands on his hips waiting for an answer. When it was clear he wasn't going to get one, he threw them in the air. The moment had passed.

SNAP.

Charley fell straight to his knees and started searching the ground. "Where's my fuckin' underwear?" he said, digging his fingers into the mud. He let out a sigh of relief when he felt the nylon texture of his shorts and practically jumped into them as soon as he stood up.

"Don't you think you're over-reacting?" Mike said, rubbing Charley's back while he fastened his drawstrings. "There's nobody else out here but us."

"Listen, you might want people to know you're a fa—" Charley stopped before he could say it, he knew it would hurt Mike's feelings "—that you're different. But I don't. So, let's just forget this whole thing."

Before Mike could answer, Charley barged past him, nearly knocking him back to the ground again. He raced through the gaps in the trees, hoping that what minimal moonlight there was would guide him back to the lake.

How could you be so stupid? he thought, huffing like a bull. *What would Dad say if you got caught again, huh?* Charley shuddered. No siree, that was one smack to the face he didn't want to experience again. He could take a punch from any other guy, but not from Mr. Reiner.

Sweat poured down Charley's back, and his breaths grew heavier into a jagged panting. To stop himself throwing up, he leaned against a tree and tried to slow his breathing down. He couldn't control the vomit once it made its way up his chest though and hunched down to spew it out. He could feel the heat of the spew on his face while he coughed out the last few chunks, and then the smell hit his nose. Those damn sloppy joes.

"CHARLEY!"

Charley stiffened up, listening for Mike's screams in the distance. "Mike?"

"HELP ME! CHARLEY! PLEASE!"

After the second scream Charley didn't hesitate. He ran through the trees, feet crashing into the mud. The closer he got, Mike's pleas got more desperate. Along the way he bashed into trees and branches, letting them scratch at the skin on his arms and his face. He ran until he couldn't run anymore.

The screams stopped.

"Mike!" he cried out, so loud that his voice became hoarse, still stinging from the vomit. "Where are you? Mike!"

Nothing. Not a sound.

Charley stood still, shifting his eyes from every direction

around him. He was lost. All he could see was the blackness. But someone was there. He could feel it. Someone was with him. He spun in a circle, searching for them until it occurred to him there was one place he hadn't looked.

Up.

Charley didn't even have a chance to look. Before he could raise his head, he was hovering over the ground, a sharp pain digging into his torso.

He kicked and screamed for his life.

PART ONE

40 YEARS LATER...

CHAPTER I

REBEL, REBEL

It was the final straw for everyone involved.

Brody Jackson's mother, father, principal, and peer worker—they were all sick of him and his destructive behavior. At only eighteen, Brody managed to build up a terrifyingly impressive résumé in criminal activity. Property damage, breaking and entering, theft, and his most recent addition, arson. He didn't need to be told by anyone that this time he had screwed up—well and truly—for the last time. He thought for sure he would be sent away to prison this time. That's what his defense was telling him anyway.

As he waited for the hearing to take place, Brody sat, leg bouncing up and down while he stared into the weak coffee on the table. He imagined what he would say if he was called upon—what could he say? *I wish I could lie to you all and say I come from a broken home, that I got in with the wrong crowd, that I was just a lost soul who needed guidance.* Yeah, it all sounded very much like a Lifetime Original in his head, but the reality was that nobody would believe him. Not this time.

It had been a month since Brody set fire to his high school, right after he was expelled. "Call it rage or anger—call it petty if you want to—I don't give a shit," he said to Mr. Fairhurst, his defense attorney, during their first meeting. "Believe it or not, I was trying to finish school with good grades and good recommendations, but my principal would never let me be anything but a 'thug'. That's what he called me, by the way."

Mr. Fairhurst nodded. He was a balding man, around mid-forties and the bags under his eyes suggested he'd seen a lot of shit in his time. He listened as Brody told his side of the story, scribbling notes on his pad and occasionally humming as he did so. "I believe there was a theft, wasn't there? Some missing money that led to your expulsion?"

"Yeah." Brody sighed. "From the school accounts, apparently. I never stole that money. I'm no tech geek, that's not my specialty. It was an obvious setup from the principal. Payback for all the hassle I caused him over the years. And of course, to get me out of school for good. That I take no responsibility for."

More humming from Mr. Fairhurst. He never gave anything away about what he really thought. Reading his face was like reading The Bible. Made no sense. Brody studied his face to see if there was anything—a sharp glance, a twitch of the eyebrow—but he was like a robot. In a way it suited Brody fine. All anyone else had done so far was throw the book at him or try to manipulate him with their sympathy. The only person's opinion that mattered to him was his mom's, but even she wouldn't take his calls anymore.

He'd tried to convince his mom—begged her, in fact—to hear him out. She shook her head when the police cuffed him and tried to stay strong, but it didn't stop the tears from falling from her eyes. "I can't do this anymore."

Brody stared at his mother, ashamed of himself for making her feel that way, until the police dragged him away.

It was the last time he would see his home once his sentence was decided.

Mr. Fairhurst was better in action than Brody anticipated. Clearly, a courtroom was where he allowed himself to come alive, because it was the first time Mr. Fairhurst showed an ounce of personality and emotion. He made a sympathetic case for Brody. It was just unfortunate the judge assigned to the case was Judge Phillips. Someone Brody was certain would be pissed at seeing him in his courtroom. Again. There would be no winning with that sour face involved. Even though Brody hid behind a moody, adolescent scowl, he was terrified of going away. He didn't know what to expect.

But the judge made his decision. And to everyone's surprise, especially his own, Brody wasn't to be sent away to a jail.

"The state of California has had it up to here with young kids like yourself who have no respect for the law," Judge Phillips said before he passed down his judgment. He leaned over the bench and burned his eyes into Brody. "You have one more chance, Mr. Jackson. A chance to redeem yourself. I'm sentencing you to one year at a reform facility to prove you can be an outstanding citizen to society."

Judge Phillips slammed the gavel. Brody jolted from the loud bang that echoed around the courtroom. It was like someone had just fired a gun.

"Don't make me regret my decision," Judge Phillips said, narrowing his eyes.

Brody eyed Mr. Fairhurst while the judge continued talking. He was confused, of course, what that meant initially. Sensing his anxiety, and without taking his eyes off Judge Phillips, Mr. Fairhurst shuffled some of the papers in front of him and slid a flyer across the table to Brody.

CAMP SILVER OAKS
A place for redemption and forgiveness

Feeling lost? Feeling like there's no way back from your mistakes? Praying for a miracle?
Silver Oaks Corrections Camp is here to help you reform!

The flyer was filled with ridiculous pictures of goody-goody young men and women, dressed like kids from a sleepaway camp, all raft-building, canoeing, and sitting with an acoustic guitar by a campfire. Brody wasn't fooled by the obvious models used in the fancy advertising. He also wasn't convinced by the message in general. The whole thing reminded him of conversion therapy propaganda. He'd watched enough conspiracy videos on YouTube to recognize such a con.

"Is this a fucking joke?" Brody whispered to Mr. Fairhurst, grinning. "They're seriously sending me away to sing *Kumbaya* around a campfire for a year like a first grader?"

Mr. Fairhurst sighed, clearly exhausted by Brody and the whole case. His job was done. Brody knew he was hard work and that he didn't exactly make it easy for Mr. Fairhurst. Or himself. He knew Mr. Fairhurst was glad the whole thing was over and that he didn't have to see Brody again.

"It's no joke," he said sternly. "You got very lucky, Brody. Do yourself a favor and remember that."

Mr. Fairhurst stood up, shoving his files back into his briefcase. He went to leave but hesitated before he placed a firm hand on Brody's shoulder. "It's no walk in the park either. Make no mistake about it, this isn't a vacation."

He gave Brody a weak smile before he finally walked away.

Brody looked down at the fake-as-fuck flyer once again. "It

sure as hell looks like one." He mumbled and tossed it aside.

The guards collected Brody and told him he was to be escorted to the camp right away. He turned around to see his parents sitting at the back of the courtroom. His dad sat with his arms crossed, seemingly disinterested in the fact he wouldn't see his son for at least a year. Brody scoffed. His dad was only there as support for his mom, who sat as still as a statue. There was nothing in her face, no welling in the eyes, she just stared ahead as if Brody wasn't even there.

Once he was out of the courtroom, Brody thought about his mom and how she used to be his biggest supporter and defender. She was the reason why he tried to change and become a better person. He was doing well in school and even managed to get most of his teachers on his side by working hard and applying himself. Brody proved he could do it—because he knew he could do it—that he could be someone else, that he could change. But it was one last screw-up too many to his mother. His dad gave up on him a long time ago. It broke Brody's heart to see the way his mom looked. Like he was the biggest disappointment—and regret—of her entire life.

*

Right after the hearing, the guards escorted Brody to the back entrance of the courthouse. The guards talked among themselves while Brody stood between them inhaling their cigarette smoke. He wasn't much of a smoker himself, only socially, but now more than ever he craved a drag. Still, he was grateful for the fresh air, and time to reflect on his verdict. He couldn't get his head around the concept of Camp Silver Oaks and all it claimed to be. He'd never heard of anyone going to such a place.

Snapping out of his thoughts, Brody listened to the guard on his left, a bald red-faced dude, brag about his 'hot date' with Sandra on reception—whoever she was—while the other guard, a pretty boy with designer stubble, nodded frantically just as he was getting to the juicy details.

"I'm sorry to interrupt this, erm, *stimulating* conversation," Brody said, crossing his brows, "but I was wondering if you guys had ever heard of Camp Silver Oaks?"

Baldie stared him down for a moment. "No," he said, focusing back on other guard. "So, I said to Sandra, 'Have you got a bit of Irish in you?', and then I said, 'Would you like —"

Brody zoned out from the macho talk when he saw a faded yellow car drive through the gates. He wasn't an expert on cars or brands, but it was old, battered and one road bump away from ending up at the junkyard. The driver stuck a hand out the window, flashing some form of documentation between their fingers and the tender raised the barrier into the backlot. Pretty Boy spotted the car too and quickly flicked his cigarette away, proceeding to stand with a straight back.

"Okay, princess," Baldie said, grabbing Brody by the arm a little bit harder than was necessary, "your date's here."

"Who, Sandra?" Brody smirked to hide his fear.

"Shut your mouth, kid," Pretty Boy said through gritted teeth.

"Where's the van?" Brody asked.

Neither of the guards answered, just stared ahead as the car pulled up, turning off its sick-sounding motor. The smell of gasoline lingered around Brody's nose. It wasn't a cigarette, but he enjoyed the rush it gave him. His moment of joy was ruined when he was dragged to the car. Baldie fished through his belt until he retrieved a key which he held up in front of

Brody, leaning down to look him in the eyes.

"No funny business," he said. "I take these off, you get straight into the car. Understand?"

Brody smirked back. "Yep. Oh, how I hate goodbyes."

The guard gripped him by the wrist, yanking him forward and unlocked the cuffs. As soon as he was free, Brody massaged the faint red circles on his wrists and inhaled in the last remnants of cigarette smoke. Pretty Boy already had the backdoor of the car open for him and rested a hand on Brody's head to help him into the vehicle.

Brody spun his head round before he entered. "Wait—what about my things?"

"You won't be needing them," the guard said, placing his hand back on Brody's head, pushing him inside the car.

There were no mesh windows in the car, or even a mesh barrier between the back and front of the vehicle. Despite the torn fabric on the seats, being held together by duct tape, it smelled pleasant unlike the van he arrived at the courthouse in. That one stunk of strong body odor and urine and Brody had felt it sinking into his skin. Content with his surroundings, Brody looked ahead as the driver turned in his seat and flashed him a smile. He was surprisingly young, in his early-twenties at most.

"It's nice to meet you, Brody," he said, white teeth gleaming between his chubby cheeks.

Brody didn't return the gesture.

"Yo," he mumbled, before turning his attention to the seatbelt and feeling around the seat for a buckle.

Not fazed by Brody's disinterest, the driver didn't make any effort to turn around and watched Brody struggle with the belt for a moment before he said, "I'm Bart, by the way."

Brody fluttered his eyes. "Is your last name Simpson, too, or would that just be *too much* of a coincidence?"

"It is Simpson, just FYI," Bart said.

There was an awkward silence.

Bart eventually let out a belly laugh. "Oh, he's a joker. I think we're going to get along just fine."

After fighting with the seatbelt, Brody managed to buckle himself in and let out a long sigh. In the corner of his eye Bart was still smiling at him, but Brody chose to look out the window instead of facing him again. "So, are you, like, an Uber driver or something?"

"No, I'm one of your camp counselors."

Brody scoffed. "My *what*?"

"Didn't you read the flyer?"

Brody leaned his head back into the seat. "Enough to know it's a freakshow."

"We'll talk along the way. We have a long drive ahead." Bart turned back in his seat and glanced at Brody in the rear-view mirror. "There's some more flyers in the back, somewhere, if you want to read more about it."

Brody closed his eyes, unable to remember the last time he got a decent night's sleep since his arrest. "I think I'll pass," he said, which prompted Bart to finally stop talking to him and start up the engine. As soon as he did, there was a sickly strain in the pit of Brody's stomach. The moment had come and there was nothing he could do about it now, he accepted that. But it still didn't stop him from wanting to leap out of the car and make a run for it while he could. Of course, it would be useless.

I always get caught, anyways.

One of the guards banged on the roof, giving Bart the go ahead to leave the premises. The car started to move, which only fueled Brody with more dread. He kept telling himself, *It's only for a year. It's only for a year.*

"Do you like music?" Bart asked, interrupting Brody's prep talk to himself. "I made a playlist for the trip."

Although he wasn't in the mood for Bart's perky—and annoying—enthusiasm, Brody decided to play along. "Sure," he said, with his eyes closed.

"Do you like Stevie Nicks?"

"*Love* him."

Bart giggled. "Lamest joke in history."

"Who's joking?"

Brody opened his eyes and watched Bart push a cassette tape into the car stereo. The car really was ancient. *Edge of Seventeen* crackled from the poor-quality speakers, at a louder volume than it needed to be. Brody found himself tapping his foot to the beat after a while.

At some point, he managed to drift off.

＊

Brody squinted out the window, surprised how bright it was outside. In the front Bart was humming another 80s classic—*Eyes Without a Face* by Billy Idol. It was on a playlist Brody had on his phone. He put his hand in his pocket, searching around for it. And then he remembered.

Oh yeah.

He thought the effects of going cold turkey with his digital detox would have worn off by now, but no. The nap did him no good. It only made him more exhausted, and it was a restless nap, at that. Mostly because of everything running around in his head, but also because the car seat was extremely uncomfortable. He rubbed at the back of his neck, attempting to massage it.

Bart locked eyes with him in the rear-view and greeted him with a smile that stretched across his eyes. "Hey, he's awake! I was starting to get lonely up here."

"Aw," Brody mumbled, continuing to rub his neck and stretch his back. "Bless your heart."

"Bad sleep, huh?"

Jesus, does he ever shut up?

"I've had better."

Outside there were vast empty fields. Brody had never seen this part of the state before, of course, if they were even in the state anymore. The wind from Bart's window blew in a mixed scent of freshly cut grass and horseshit. That woke him up. Despite the smell, there were no animals on the fields. He also took note that their car was the only one on the road. Wherever Brody was, it seemed totally isolated from the world he had just left behind.

Bart tapped on the stirring wheel, shifting his gaze between the road and the rear-view mirror. Obviously, he was trying to find something—anything—to talk to Brody about. He still wasn't in the mood for conversation, but it was better to rip the Band-Aid off himself. "So, this Camp Silver Oaks place, what is it? What's the catch?"

Bart shrugged. "Well, it's just a campsite, with cabins, canoeing and—"

"No," Brody said. "I'm asking what it *really* is. You can't tell me that it's going to be all fresh air, acoustic guitars, and marshmallows by the fire every night."

For a moment Bart considered the question. "Well, yeah, kinda," he said. "Redeeming yourself doesn't need to be an unpleasant experience. The idea is that you reform your character. What better way to do that than by spending it doing team activities and getting to know others who have overcome their mistakes? There is no catch—it's exactly what it says it is."

Brody shook his head. "Bullshit. You know what I did, don't you? They don't send people like me to somewhere that isn't unpleasant."

"Well, you're wrong," Bart said, with a bit of a bite in his voice. "I think Silver Oaks is exactly what you need. Being in an environment like that can only do you the world of good. No internet, no phone, no excuse to get into any trouble. Everyone loves it there. Trust me, you will too."

Bart flicked his eyes away from the mirror and back on the road, frowning as he did so. His pitch was good, but Brody still wasn't convinced.

*

Bart drove for over an hour without saying anything else. The volume of the music had crept up a notch as a substitute for the silence between him and Brody. The sun was still quite high in the sky and blared through the windows. Brody tugged at his shirt collar and wiped at the fresh sweat on his neck. It was still hot despite the heavy wind coming through the window. Without his phone, or even his watch, it was hard to tell what time it was, but he guessed it was probably well into late afternoon. His stomach started to rumble, and his mouth was dry from the heat. There was no sign of a gas station at all, but even if there was one, he doubted Bart would agree to stop.

The awkward silence between him and Bart became unbearable after a while. And Brody couldn't listen to anymore of Bart's humming. "So, if you're a counselor, why did you drive all that way to pick me up?"

Bart quickly adjusted the volume on his stereo. "Silver Oaks is a special case. We always pick up new campers ourselves."

Brody responded with a snort.

"What?' Bart said, smiling and furrowing his brows at the same time.

"Honestly, Bartholomew…*campers*?"

"Well, it's more endearing than the alternative term, isn't it? And it's just Bart, thank you *very* much."

The comment wiped the smirk off Brody's face. He didn't need to ask Bart what the alternative term was—he knew full well what being a camper really meant. But his question was food for thought. They could dress Silver Oaks up however they liked. At the end of the day, Brody was a prisoner. Locked away and isolated. And without any of his devices, not only would he be unable to see what was going on in the world, he was going to be dead to it, too.

Bart glanced at Brody in the mirror. "We'll be there soon," he said, smiling and turning the music back up—*Kids in America* by Kim Wilde. Although it was his comment that brought Brody spiraling back down to reality, Bart's smile was comforting.

*

Bart kept his promise and twenty minutes later they drove down a long road surrounded by large oak trees. At the end of the road, they came to a large frame made from tree trunks which—to Brody's surprise—had no gate. The area around the entrance was surrounded by a row of tall oaks that seemed to go on for miles. Brody leaned forward to peer out the window at the large sign before them, made from logs and coated in faded red paint:

CAMP SILVER OAKS

"Here it is," Bart said. "Home."

CHAPTER II

THE CAMP

Bart drove past the entrance where the trees started to clear from either side of the pathway. Eventually all that could be seen was the land that the camp occupied. Brody couldn't believe it, but now he was able to witness it with his own eyes. Camp Silver Oaks, on the surface, really did look like an actual summer camp. Not that Brody had ever been to one, but he'd watched enough horror movies to know the ins-and-outs of such a place. The central area was littered with rustic red cabins that looked a little weathered. But the early evening sun made them appear vibrant. Further down the path there was a larger building, painted in green with a carved wooden sign above it:

MESS HALL

A couple of the so-called 'campers' rested on the frames around the porch of the mess hall. They glanced over at Bart's car with a mixture of grins and general curiosity. Brody glared back at the campers as they started to talk among themselves. He expected them to look a little more roughed-up, but to his surprise they looked just like the people photographed for the flyer. It was fucking weird. Mostly, he was drawn to what they were wearing. They were dressed just like kids at a summer camp and, considering the age of them, their attire made them look like the cast of some 80s slasher flick. The standard uniform was a grey t-shirt or sweater with **CAMP SILVER OAKS** printed in bold capital letters. Some of the campers were creative enough to style them in different ways. One guy had rolled up the sleeves and another had cut them off completely. The campers added to the look with high white tube socks that had three red stripes, paired with white or black Converse. Then finally, much to Brody's horror, black short-shorts with white piping. They really were going for that retro vibe.

Bart stopped the car just outside the mess hall and turned off the engine. As soon as he did, Brody took his seatbelt off and leaned forward. "There is absolutely *no fucking way* that I am wearing those shorts, just so we're clear."

Even with his back turned to him, Brody could tell by the jolt in Bart's shoulders that he found his comment hilarious. Without saying anything, Bart got out of the car and tried to hide his grin. His red face gave him away.

Brody knocked on the window to gain his attention again. "I'm not joking!" he said through the glass. Bart shook his head and made his way over to a group of people standing by a cabin further down the path. This one wasn't red like the others, but a chipped off-white.

Now that he could see Bart fully, he stood out from everyone else. He was dressed in a pair of ripped jeans and a faded t-shirt with David Bowie on it from his Ziggy Stardust days. The rest of the group were dressed like the campers too, with the exception that their t-shirts were red instead of grey. There were six of them in total—three men and three women that looked slightly older than the campers he'd seen so far. Brody assumed they were the other camp counselors and observed Bart as he shook their hands and pointed toward the car. They all looked over and offered a small wave at Brody. He returned their gesture with a scowl.

As the counselors talked among themselves, they stopped when a man dressed in a white shirt and black slacks emerged from the white cabin. He looked around forty or fifty, with harsh circles under his wide eyes and sported a cropped salt-and-pepper hairstyle. He spread his arms and smiled at Bart before the man embraced him in a quick hug. It wasn't hard to figure out that this dude was the big boss. The other counselors turned their attention to him as he started to talk away. There was a lot of nodding going on from his listeners, and a lot of smiling. Teeth showing and eyes popping out of their heads, hanging on to his every word. *Who is this guy? Jesus or something?* He took a break from talking when he made eye contact with Brody.

The man bowed his head at him, followed by a wide grin. *Creep.*

Brody continued to observe the conversation, trying to lip-read as best he could. It was obvious they were talking about him, but he couldn't quite work out the gist of the conversation.

Absorbed by trying to figure out what they were saying, Brody's ass jumped off the seat when there was a knock on the window. He jumped so high that he banged his head on the roof of the car.

"Jesus!" he yelled, rubbing the top of his head.

There was a knock on the window once again—with more force this time. All Brody could see outside now was a long torso and the waistband of some shorts. He rolled at the stiff plastic handle to open the window and popped his head out to face the long-bodied boy.

"What?" Brody asked, frowning.

The boy was tall—at least six feet—and looked like he belonged in an *Abercrombie & Fitch* store. He too seemed a little older than the other campers and Brody, but it was probably just his height. His sharp chiseled jaw was scattered with some patches of short stubble, so he was still growing into his manhood.

The tall boy leaned down to greet Brody with a lazy smile. One that was smug and self-aware. "I'm Luke," he said. "I'm supposed be showing you around."

Brody didn't move and just stared back at the guy, thinking—and hoping—that he would eventually look away or piss off. Luke wasn't fazed or intimidated. He waited patiently for Brody to either get out the car or respond. Brody had always been good at scaring people off by staring them out, but it was clear it didn't work on this dude.

"Lucky, lucky me…" Brody said, bobbing his head from side-to-side. "Well, are you gonna stand there or are you gonna get the door?"

Luke grabbed the handle and pulled the door open so quick that—judging by the loud creaking noise it made—Brody thought he had ripped it off its hinges. But that was probably just the age of the vehicle. Seriously, Bart needed some new wheels.

Brody sighed and got out the car as gracefully as possible. His legs felt like jelly from sitting in the same position for so long which made him stumble over. *Smooth, Brody, smooth.* He was glad Luke had already marched ahead so nobody saw the embarrassing display. Luke, in his smugness, must have assumed Brody would follow him.

And he did.

"So, what's your name?" Luke asked as he paced on.

Brody knew full well he already knew what it was because he was told to show him around. "Whatever you want it to be, *big boy*."

Luke stopped.

At first Brody was grateful because he was already out of breath. But then Luke hunched his shoulders like *The Hulk* and spun around in a flash. Before he knew it, Luke stormed his way back over to him. Not knowing what to expect, Brody clenched his fist ready to take the first swing if he even attempted to get any closer.

Luke's eyes went straight to Brody's clenched fist. He stood across from him and folded his arms, raising an eyebrow. "Are you going to be a problem?"

He tried not to laugh but Brody couldn't stop himself from smirking. How could he take him seriously, especially when he was trying to be authoritative, in those shorts?

Luke's face started to burn red. "What's so funny?"

"Jesus, dude, take a joke. My name is Brody," he said, extending his hand. "Mr. Jackson if ya nasty." Wink.

Luke didn't unfold his arms, but the color flushed away from his cheeks. He looked Brody up and down. "Nice to meet you, Brody," he muttered, then turned away and carried on marching ahead.

Brody rolled his eyes and followed Luke once again.

*

Luke gave Brody a tour of the grounds, not that there was anything he didn't expect to see at a campsite. It wasn't a hard place to navigate, that was the point. After all, Silver Oaks was nothing more than a dressed-up prison, so it wasn't as if they would want their prisoners to go far or be out of sight. What played on his mind the most was the lack of security or gate. What was to stop him from walking out in the middle of the night?

"So where are the blind spots?" Brody asked when Luke showed him the art room which was sat just behind the mess hall.

Luke blinked once. "*What?*"

"Ya know, places to avoid the CCTV?"

"There is no CCTV."

Brody grinned. "Even better!"

Luke leaned in close enough that Brody could smell his breath. Minty fresh. "We don't need it. Make no mistake, we see all. Don't try anything stupid."

"Wasn't gonna…"

Luke wasn't the most enthusiastic of tour guides and Brody wondered if he was giving the place the justice it deserved. Luke only gave him some quick, abbreviated commentary:

"Here's the mess hall. We eat here."

"That's where we have campfires and sing songs. No, I'm not joking. Why would I be joking?"

"This is where we play baseball. I'm sure you could do with the exercise."

Brody took a particular interest in the archery range, located on the field just opposite the mess hall. Mostly because it made him want to poke Luke's eyes out and stop his monotone droning. But also, it piqued his curiosity. If this was a prison, why were they letting them play with bows and arrows? Seemed like an accident waiting to happen.

Luke guided Brody down a path that led to a dock in front of the lake. Some of the campers were putting away the canoes and piling up their self-made rafts by the waterfront. The lake was surrounded by beautiful tall trees and went round in a never-ending bend. From the dock, the pink sun was nearly all the way down for the day and reflected on the ripples of the water. The view was spectacular, Brody had to admit that. Several campers passed them by and Brody couldn't help but notice how happy they all seemed. He couldn't tell if it was genuine or if their happiness was just as artificial as the Silver Oaks flyer.

One of the female counselors that Brody saw earlier stood near the steps of the dock, giving him a once-over before smiling at him and Luke.

"You must be our new camper,' she said, extending her hand. "I'm Pamela, one of your counselors."

"Brody." He shook her hand and turned toward the dock.

Pamela didn't let go of Brody's hand, though, and yanked him back when he went to approach the steps up to the dock. Brody pulled his hand away from Pamela, ready to ask her what the hell she was doing. But she turned away from him before he could. "Luke, it's nearly dinner time," she said. "Maybe you should show Brody to his cabin? If you haven't already."

Luke nodded and waved his hand for Brody to follow him. Before Brody left, he squinted at Pamela and rubbed his shoulder.

What a bitch.

"Run along now," she said.

Brody sped up his walk to catch up to Luke. Once they were up the path, he turned around again to see Pamela standing there watching them leave.

Waiting.

"What's her problem?" Brody whispered.

Luke shrugged. "What do you mean?"

"She pretty much pulled my arm out of my socket when I tried to step on that dock. Are they all like that?"

"You're new. She's just being cautious, that's all."

"Cautious of what? I just wanted to look at the view."

Luke ignored him and pointed ahead once they were back at the camp. "That's us over there—Cabin 12."

Us?

Luke led the way to the cabin. There was nothing special that distinguished it from the other red cabins around it. Except for the number 12 on the door. Inside, the cabin walls were lined with smooth wooden planks that matched the bed frames. There were six beds in total, with a small unit of three drawers next to each bed. It was very bare, just as Brody expected it to be.

"That's your bed," Luke said, pointing to the one in the far corner dressed in the same baby-blue sheets as the others.

On the end of Brody's bed was a pile of neatly folded clothes. The camp uniform. Brody eyed the shorts and cringed at the thought of wearing them. Very 1980s. Brody wiped his sweaty brow. The air inside the cabin was so humid and so stale, that the shorts suddenly didn't seem that unappealing.

"This is my cabin too," Luke said, "so we'll be rooming together." There was a distaste in his tone, which didn't go unnoticed by Brody. "I think this would be a good time to go over some expectations."

"Wait—*expectations*?" Brody said, snorting. "It's a cabin. I think I get the idea."

Luke proceeded. "Your bed should always be made when you're not in it, you should always be hygienic and—" he stopped to give Brody a once-over "—well groomed. You must always wear your camp uniform, so you may as well get rid of your clothes. You won't be needing them anymore."

Brody cocked his head to one side. "Except for when I get out of here, I'll be needing them then," he said. "So, I'll keep hold of them until then. Thanks."

Luke carried on. "In your storage unit, you have plenty of spares to wear. Sweaters and sweatpants for when it gets cold. Always be respectful to everyone—*that includes your fellow campers.*" He emphasized that last point. "No smoking, drinking or drugs. Any contraband can get you—and others—into serious trouble with—"

"With you?" Brody said, snickering.

"Yes, and the camp counselors. All meals are to be eaten in the mess hall. If you have a medical emergency, the counselors rotate at the infirmary inside the main office—"

"What are you in for?" Brody interrupted, again, bored of his rambling.

Luke hardened his face. "And never ask another camper why they're here. It's forbidden."

Forbidden? Brody wondered. What kind of bullshit was that? Surely Luke was just making up his own rules now. Either way, it didn't bother Brody much. He didn't particularly care to make friends with anyone.

They stood awkwardly for a moment until Luke broke the silence. "Dinner is in about thirty minutes. The shower block is two cabins down," he said, twitching his nose. "No time like the present."

Before Brody could come back with a smart remark, Luke spun on his heels and left the cabin.

Alone, and with nobody else about, Brody took his nose to his pit and breathed in the scent. He didn't smell *too* bad. "Weirdo..." he said toward the door. Looking around at his new home, Brody sat on the edge of his bed and took in the silence.

"Well, it could be worse," he sighed, "I could be sharing with Pamela."

*

The shower block had seen better days. A concrete row of showerheads that spurted cold water like a dribbling mouth. The cubicles were separated by worn-down and water damaged plaster boards that looked ready to collapse, too.

After his shower, Brody made his way to the mess hall, tugging at the front of his t-shirt, which was just a bit too tight and a bit too short. He hated having his belly button exposed and sucked his stomach in to hide the few pounds of weight he hadn't wanted to admit he'd put on.

Jesus, were these clothes designed for kids or something?

Brody lingered on the porch of the mess hall for a moment, adjusting the waist band of his shorts to try and cover his stomach. He listened to the laughter and chatter echoing from inside. He felt like an impostor in the camp uniform, and absolutely ridiculous, of course. *It's just for one year. Just do as they say, do what they want and make Mom proud.* Easier said than done. He peeped through one of the windows, watching as the campers laughed, talked and shoveled inhumanly large amounts of food into their mouths. The scene reminded Brody of high school, they seemed to have their own groups and cliques. And just like high school, he was content to not participate or join any of them.

All he wanted to do was go to sleep, he was past being hungry, but he knew he had to eat something. His mind was made up. He'd go in, grab a snack, and go straight back out as soon as he was done. It was inevitable that he would be the center of attention, but it was best to get it over and done with.

As soon as Brody walked in, he was greeted by nods, smiles, waves, and curious glances of the strangers around him. He made no attempt to grace them with the same curtesy and kept his head high all the way to the serving station. The cook looked like she was closing the kitchen for the night, but there was plenty of food wrapped on the counter.

"Hi, it's Brody, isn't it?" she said, wiping her hands with a dirty cloth. She was an older woman, probably in her late fifties. Strings of grey hair framed her round face, escaping from her hairnet.

He nodded.

"Take whatever you want. It's probably cold by now, but I can heat it up if—"

"No thanks." Brody picked up a burger that might as well have been charcoal, and a handful of concrete fries. "Looks delicious."

Next to the station there was an empty bench where he sat to tuck into his meal, hoping he was invisible to everyone by now. Between mouthfuls of his burger, he caught some of the campers staring and whispering. On one of the middle benches, he spotted Luke with a bunch of other boys who talked to one another while Luke ate in silence. Until he locked eyes with Brody.

Brody didn't shift his focus away from him, and Luke accepted it as a challenge by resting his chin between flexed fingers. In any other place he would have simply said, "What the fuck are you staring at?", but it was probably best he let it go and not make a scene on his first evening.

Giving up on the chewy burger, Brody was ready to leave.

He grabbed his plate, about to stand until he saw Bart—now dressed in his red Camp Silver Oaks t-shirt and shorts—make his way over to the bench. He fitted in nicely with the rest of the clones now, and certainly looked the part. Yet, Brody couldn't help admiring Bart's physique now that it was on full display. He had a thick body and muscular legs, something he hadn't noticed earlier, scattered with dark blond hairs. He hated to admit it, but Bart looked good in the uniform.

Maybe it was the shorts. The obvious bulge.

"Hey, you," Bart said, bringing Brody out of his daydream. "Want some company?"

Before he could say no, Bart sat down and made himself comfortable. He rested his hands on the table and noticed how his arms popped out of his t-shirt. They weren't muscular like his legs, but broad.

Stop it, Brody.

"I was just about to go to bed actually," he said, faking a yawn.

"Oh." Bart nodded toward his food. "Are you gonna eat that?"

It was beyond Brody why anyone would want to, but Bart's face told a different story. He pushed the plate to him. "Rather you than me."

Bart ripped a bite from the burger and chewed it several times. His eyes watered from satisfaction as the meat slid down his throat. He made it look so tasty that, for a moment, Brody wondered what was in it.

"You know, you should really think about starting to make some friends here." Bart turned around and looked in Luke's direction. "Luke's a great guy, plus he's one of your cabin buddies. He'll be a good influence on you."

42

"Hmm," Brody mumbled, crossing his brows. "I don't need any friends and I don't need anyone to influence me."

"So, what? You're just gonna sit in a corner alone for the next year?" Bart said, between another mouthful. "Everything here is built around teamwork and bonding. You'll need to get along with people sooner or later."

Brody rubbed his forehead, dragging his thumb hard enough across his skin for it to burn slightly. He could feel the heaviness under his eyelids—he was tired, and he was tired of talking bullshit for the day. "Look, I can get along with people just fine. I just don't need to make friends with Patrick Bateman over there," he said, pointing directly at Luke.

"Fair enough," Bart said, getting up to leave. "Tomorrow's a brand-new day, I'm sure you'll feel better after some rest."

"Wait, before you go, there's something I need to ask."

Bart took it as an invitation to sit back down. "Sure, go ahead."

"How do I call my mom? I know I just got here, but is there payphone or something?"

Bart sighed. His cheery face became glum and heavy. "Erm, I'm sorry, Brody, but there's no phone calls allowed here. That goes for everyone. Even me, unless I'm on the road."

Brody clenched his fist under the table so hard that he dug his nails in his skin. "Why not?"

"Uncle John's rules, I'm afraid."

Brody sneered. "Uncle John? Who the fuck is Uncle John? And why does he have such a creepy name?"

"Hey!" Bart snapped, pointing his finger in Brody's face. "Watch the language and have some respect." Wiping away the frown on his pink face, Bart turned to point at the man he was talking to earlier, sat with some of the other counselors. By the look on the man's face, he had been watching them for a while. It also seemed like he'd been listening to them, even though he was on the other side of the room.

As Brody stared right into his hollow eyes, the man greeted Brody with a bow of the head—for the second time that day.

"That's Uncle John," Bart said. "He's the camp leader."

*

Brody left the mess hall not long after his conversation with Bart. The night's sky had cloaked itself over the camp with a blueish haze while the lights from each cabin glowed in the darkness. He approached Cabin 12 with his hand inches away from the door, but he heard laughter inside. Brody hadn't even considered his 'cabin buddies', as Bart referred to them. Not only was he tired, but he wasn't in the mood to make any more formal introductions. It had been a hell of a day.

It was a beautiful night, and the idea of going for a walk alone seemed appealing. He walked back through the main path between all the cabins, past the mess hall where campers were leaving for the night. They all greeted Brody with a smile, a "Hi" or 'Hello", which he amicably repeated, hoping they didn't try to stop him for a chat. He couldn't understand how everyone looked so happy and could be so friendly in this place—this *prison*. Brody wasn't happy, he was angry. Angry about the whole thing. It finally hit him that this camp would be his home now for a whole three hundred and sixty-five days. But he wasn't angry about Silver Oaks, he was angry that he was in any form of prison.

You did set fire to your school, remember?

Yeah, he committed a serious crime, there was no getting around that.

Bored of arguing with himself, he made his way further down the path that led to the lake.

*

Despite the warm weather, the scent of damp wood tickled Brody's sinuses. It was a satisfying smell, close to what he imagined the great outdoors would smell like. The constant fresh air was one advantage of being at the camp. That, and of course, the beautiful lake. It was a big open space that was peaceful. Only the faint sound of the water and a few crickets cooing away for company. The moonlight shined down on the lake's rippling surface, making the moon look like some sort of pixelated art piece.

Brody eyed the canoes and rafts next to the dock that he saw earlier. He wondered how long it would take him to canoe his way out of this place. Not long, he guessed. But he also predicted he wouldn't make it that far. No doubt, Uncle John probably had some form of security lingering somewhere— despite what Luke said about the lack of CCTV—to prevent such an incident from happening. He just hadn't made it obvious. There was no way convicted criminals would be locked up in a place without surveillance of some sort.

As he approached the dock Brody cocked his head to the side, catching something glimmer in the moonlight. It was sat underneath the dock. He bent down, grabbing onto one of the beams above him to reach it. It was embedded in the damp mud, a metal box that looked like a giant pencil case. Once he had a firm grip on the box, it came away from the mud easily enough.

Now that he could get a better look, out from the shadows, the box just looked like a dull rusty tin. A piece of junk that had probably washed up to the mound from the lake. Still, he was curious to see if there was anything inside. The top came away with a few stiff tugs, making his fingers muddy. And of all the things that could have been inside that box, he didn't expect it to contain *that.*

An old, battered, and dirty notebook. It had a faded label, that once upon a time was probably white, where a name used to be. The water must've washed away the ink. Brody had to laugh at the sticker in the left-hand corner. A circular logo with a tent in the center. It read **HAPPY CAMPER** underneath the image.

"Jesus …" he said, shaking his head. Why would someone feel the need to put a notebook in a box? Did they throw it in the lake? Did they bury it under the dock like one of those time capsule things? It was strange, but then Brody remembered where he was. Everything here was strange.

He flicked through the notebook. Other than a few dirty pages, they weren't too damaged. The darkness made it difficult to make out any of the writing but judging by the layout, this was someone's diary. A few pages had also been torn out. Brody considered just tossing it back to the ground. What use would he have for someone else's diary? Then again, it would make some potentially interesting reading.

Why else would it be hidden?

With the notebook in hand, Brody made his way up the steps to the dock. A light breeze brushed against his skin as he walked down the stretch. Once he got to the end, he stared out into the distance for a moment. He took in the scent of the night before taking off his socks and Converse shoes and sat down to dip his feet into the water. It was ice-cold, but it felt amazing.

He started to daydream about his childhood and how his

parents never allowed him to go to a sleepaway camp or took him on any camping vacations. His mom worked long hours as a nurse, and his dad was always so tight with money that he would never splash out on a vacation—no matter how much Brody or his mom begged him.

She'd love this, he thought. *I wish you were here with me, Mom.*

Alone, he could feel the heat on his face and the lump in his throat. Brody tried to fight it, but he couldn't any longer. He'd been holding back the tears for nearly a month, and finally allowed himself to cry.

He'd let his mother down and that killed him more than anything. He wanted to call her, so he could apologize and beg for forgiveness. To hear her tell him everything would be okay. But he remembered the way she looked during his sentence, and deep down he knew that she was done with him.

He heard her voice again: *I can't do this anymore.*

The tears came to a halt when something bubbled to the surface of the lake. It was huge, exploding into the air and sending gushes of water toward him. Brody removed his feet from the surface, crawling backward as the silhouette splashed again. Jumping to his feet, he only caught a glimpse of whatever was moving.

Large. Too large for the lake.

Its dark silhouette rippled against the water before it sank back down. It looked like one giant mass, stalking him from below the surface.

"What the fuck…" he whispered, leaning over the dock, and squinting at the center of the lake.

The ripples began to settle under the moon, but they stretched out to either side of the lake. Brody considered the possibilities. An alligator? No, it was far too big. He was no David Attenborough, but he was pretty sure this wasn't gator country. Whatever it was, it scared him enough to hear his pulse through his eardrums.

Once the ripples had disappeared, he pressed his hand against his chest. His heart still pounded.

"*Brody!*"

He whipped his head round toward the wooded area behind him. It was Bart. Even in the dark, he could see his cheeks were flushed pink. He looked pissed. Brody picked up his socks, stuffing them into the waistband of his shorts, scooped up the notebook and shoved his feet into the toecap of his Converse. He took one last look at the water before Bart called his name again—his voice hoarse the second time.

At the steps to the dock, Brody looked down at Bart who was now crossing his arms. "Can't get enough of me today, huh, Simpson?"

The joke was wasted. He was clearly *too* pissed off. "What the hell do you think you're doing out here alone?"

"I came for a walk, is that a crime?"

Bart shifted his eyes to the lake. "Here it is, yes. Didn't Luke explain that you can't go wondering around alone at night—especially here?"

Brody shrugged. "Golden boy must've missed that part out," he said, jumping off the dock, nearly losing one of his shoes when he landed. "What do you think's gonna happen? I'll swim my way out of here?"

Sweat dripped down Bart's face, staining the neck of his t-shirt. Brody could practically feel the heat of the steam coming off him. "If you ever do this again, I'll write you up."

"So, you're letting me off with a warning?" Brody said,

placing a hand over his mocking, wide open mouth. "Isn't that favoritism?"

The shock of Bart grabbing his arm—with a little more force than was necessary—made Brody want to swing for him. If it had been anyone else, he would have. Square in the jaw.

Bart pulled him in close, tightening his grip. "I'm not fucking around, Brody! Don't ever come out here alone again. Understand?" The insistence in his voice was frightening. He slowed his breathing and released Brody's arm.

Taking a step back, Brody rubbed at the flesh where he could feel a burn forming from the friction. Bart looked down at his other hand where he was holding the notebook.

"What've you got there?" Bart said, narrowing his eyes.

"A notebook," Brody spat, not planning to explain where he got it from. "To write down some poems. Is that a crime too?"

Brody was no poet—or a writer—but Bart didn't even question it. "Come on," he sighed, "let's go back."

Brody took the lead, knocking his shoulder into Bart on the way past. He half expected to be written up for that—whatever that even meant—but Bart didn't say anything, just followed behind him as they made their way back to the camp in silence.

*

The walk back to the cabin felt longer than it should have. Brody picked up the speed, brooding all the way back. Even at a distance, it felt like Bart was breathing down his neck. It truly felt like he hadn't had a break from the guy since he arrived, and he was starting to show his true colors behind those rosy cheeks and his happy 80s-themed humming. Once they were at Cabin 12, Brody went straight for the doorknob. The boys were still up, laughing away, but that stopped as soon as he turned the knob.

"Brody, wait," Bart said, before he could open the door. He hesitated for a moment and tilted his head so he could just about see Bart. "I—I'm sorry. I shouldn't have been so hard on you. I know it's your first day. It's a lot of rules to take in, I understand that. Can we just forget the whole thing ever happened?"

With his back still turned, Brody could only think about the way Bart grabbed him. The yelling he could live with, but if that was a taster of things to come, he sure as shit wasn't going to forget about it a second time.

Brody took a deep breath and faced Bart. "It's forgotten."

"Thanks." Bart let out a deep breath himself. He began to sway and fidget with his hands while Brody stood waiting for him to say something else. "Well…goodnight then."

Bart walked down the path. Brody waited a moment before he decided to ask him what was on his mind in the first place. "Are there any alligators, or crocodiles, or…whatever…around here?"

"No. Why?"

"I saw something in the lake—before you came—it was pretty big."

Bart shrugged. "It was probably just a fish."

It wasn't, but he couldn't describe something he didn't *actually* see.

Brody nodded. "Yeah, probably."

Bart smiled and waved him off as Brody watched him disappear into the night. He wondered how Bart knew he was even down by the lake. Then, he wondered how someone like Bart ended up in a place like Camp Silver Oaks. An actual summer camp he could understand, kids would love Bart and bounce off his energy. To essentially be a prison guard to a bunch of criminals just didn't seem like the right role for him. But as Brody witnessed earlier, if he needed to put someone in line, he certainly could.

As much as he didn't want to, Brody couldn't wait any longer and braved meeting his roommates. Before he went in, he tucked the notebook behind his back and into the waistband of his shorts. When he opened the door, he saw that they had pushed four of the beds together and were beginning a card game. All of them—except for Luke—turned their attention away from their decks and greeted him with uncertain smiles and "Hellos". Besides Luke, there were four other boys in total.

One of them, who sported a pair of glasses that had duct tape on the bridge, stood off the bed and came over to extend his hand. "Hi Brody, I'm Josh. It's a pleasure to meet you," he said, with a faint detection of a lisp.

"Thanks," Brody said, taking his hand. He peered past Josh's head to look at the other three. "And you guys?"

Before any of them got a chance to introduce themselves, Josh did it for them and began by pointing at the red-head sat next to Luke. "That's Pete, he's allergic to nuts." Then he turned his attention to another who was dealing the cards out. "That's Akeeb, he's a mad Marvel nerd, but I promise he's cool."

Last up was a weedy-looking kid with slimy-pale skin glistening with sweat from the heat. "And this is Rich, he's an albino, but he's *our* albino. Aren't ya, Richie?"

"Hi," Rich muttered, darting his eyes away from Brody.

Josh carried on with the introductions. "And I believe you've already met Luke, haven't you?" Before Brody could say anything, Josh continued. "We're so happy to have a new cabin buddy! We're playing Liar if you want to join us?"

"You mean *Bullshit*?" Brody said to the surprise of both Josh and Luke. The others just looked at each other.

"Well, erm, we don't call it *that* here," Josh said, "but it sounds like you know how to play! Come and join us."

Brody looked over at his bed. "I'll pass, thanks."

He skirted around Josh, who frowned at his rejection. Brody noted the way Pete and Akeeb shrugged at each other, sensing his awkward reception toward them. Once he got past the beds, Brody lay down, kicked his shoes off and placed the pillow over his eyes. The others carried on playing regardless, but now that his head was down, it didn't matter. The sounds of cards snapping began to fade away.

He welcomed sleep.

*

Brody woke up to rain crashing onto the roof of the cabin. The boys were all in bed now, letting out some light snores, heavy breathing and—judging by the odor that tickled his noise—some farts too. Feeling restless, he sat up and pulled the notebook out of his waistband, away from his back. For a moment he listened to the rain, which brought him some comfort. The cabin was no cooler than it had been when he fell asleep, and he considered going outside to get some fresh air, even though he would get soaked. A strobe of lightning flashed through the window, followed by a clap of thunder. At least, it sounded like thunder the first time. But by the second time it sounded...*different*—so loud that it vibrated through the cabin.

The boys shot up from their beds, the next flash of lightning revealing their confused, sleepy faces—or were they scared?

"What the hell was that?" Brody asked the room.

No one could answer. They looked around at each other for an explanation.

Luke lay back down and turned on his side. "It's just thunder, you wimps. Go back to sleep."

"Or maybe someone's tried to run away again," Josh said.

Silence. Nobody was willing to elaborate.

"What do you mean?" Brody asked.

Turning to Brody, Josh opened his mouth to explain, but Luke beat him to it. "It's like a siren in the woods. They sound it when someone has attempted to escape in the night."

It didn't make any sense. "I've never heard of a siren that sounds like *that*," Brody said, squinting at Luke. "Like a wild animal, or something."

The thunder came around for a third time. Brody half expected something to burst through the door and tear them to pieces. He could hear Rich panting in the corner.

"Rich, put a sock in it," Luke said. "It's *just* thunder. Now can we all go back to sleep, please?"

Luke turned over again, and the others followed suit. Rich continued to pant, terrified by the noise, but tried his best to disguise it once Luke let out huge sigh. Brody stayed sitting up, awaiting the sound to come again.

*

Unable to sleep, Brody reached for the switch on the lamp next to his bed. Everyone else seemed to have drifted back to sleep. He reached for the notebook and rested it just underneath the lamp before opening it up to the first page.

"1984?" Brody whispered. "Fuck."

Another flash of lightening made him jolt. All that remained was the rain, Luke's snores, and his own heart pounding. He felt ridiculous, like he was a little kid again.

After all, it was just a bit of thunder.

It's only been a week since I arrived at Camp Stanleyside and it's an absolute **HORROR** show.

Okay, not literally, but these kids are something else. Mrs. Baker said that having a summer job would look good on my college application, although I'm starting to wonder if it's even worth it. Only this morning I asked Marla to tidy her bunk and she told me to fuck off. And of course, Darryl told me to humor it because her daddy is some rich politician. Like that means anything to me! 'Daddy' probably sent her here so he didn't have to deal with her all summer. I often wonder if it's us or even Darryl running the place. Most of time he just sits in his office—which always stinks of Mary Jane—and lets us take care of everything.

Thank God for Rusty. He always manages to get the kids to settle down when they start acting like wild animals in a zoo. And they all seem to love him, which I guess is pretty sweet. But then again, who are they going to listen to? Me, a quiet little nerd from Idaho whose only experience is babysitting her cousin? Once, might I add. Or Rusty—the cool boy from Texas who is really good at baseball, listens to cool music (**REMINDER**: buy music by The Fixx when you get home) and looks hot in footballs jerseys?

I know who I'd pick.

The other counselors are okay, I guess. Except for Tina and her two minions. Nancy and Lydia. Perfect Tina with her long blonde hair and expensive clothes from Ralph Lauren. Yesterday I caught her rolling her eyes at me when I walked over to the counselor's table at dinner. Nancy and Lydia laughed but hung their heads when they saw that I'd noticed.

"Hi," Tina said, fake as always. "We saved you a seat."

She pointed to the end of the table, right next to Andy, who had left a seat empty between himself and the other counselors.

"I think you guys have a lot in common," Tina continued. "I'm sure you'll have lots to talk about."

Because Tina laughed, it gave Nancy and Lydia permission to join in

55

again. The joke being that Andy hardly speaks. I know I'm quiet, but how he got a job as a counselor? I'll never know. I kinda feel sorry him. He's different from the others. Black hair and black clothes. He listens to this weird music a lot too. Sometimes he plays it really loud from his cabin.

Rusty was sat next to Tina. Maybe it was because he just felt sorry for me, or he could tell I was about to cry, but he stood up. "Here, you can have my seat."

Tina grabbed his arm. "Babe," she whispered, loud enough for everyone to hear. "There's already a space for her. Down there."

Rusty looked at his tray. He'd only taken one bite of his hot dog. "Yeah, I'm done. I need to take a shower anyway."

"Well, we're done too. Aren't we, girls?" Tina stood up and waited. Nancy and Lydia had barely touched their food either.

I stood there feeling even worse than before. I watched as Tina linked her arm with Rusty's, who offered me a sympathetic smile. I know girls like her, I've dealt with enough of them back home. I thought coming to Camp Stanleyside would be different. I'd have the summer to become someone else, instead of a loser.

"Table's yours," Tina said as they all walked past me.

When I sat down, Andy looked up from his tray. We locked eyes for a minute, and I couldn't read him. I didn't know if he was sad, angry, or even realized what just happened. He just carried on eating, as did the other counselors who didn't seem to care much about Tina's behavior. I lost my appetite and left.

I hope this wasn't a taste of what the rest of summer is going to be like.

I **HATE** Tina.

It seems that she wasn't too happy about Rusty giving up his seat for me at dinner last week. That night at the social, Rusty came over to me while I was getting some punch. I almost dropped my cup when I saw him standing next to me.

"Sorry, I didn't mean to scare you," he said, flashing his teeth. I hadn't noticed before, but they're kind of bucked at the front. He looked so handsome in his red check shirt. "I came over to apologize."

I knew what for, but I shrugged. "What about?"

"Tina. She can be—" he considered a word for a bit. "Well, y'know."

"A bitch?" I said, without thinking. I covered my mouth straight away. However, it made him laugh. "Yeah, pretty much."

We talked for a little bit. He asked me where I was from and what I was gonna study at college. But the conversation was cut short when Tina came over. She didn't acknowledge me.

"Oh my god, I love this song!" she said, grabbing Rusty's arm and pulling him toward the dance floor. Bananarama's _Cruel Summer_. How appropriate.

Rusty gave a small shrug. Another apology maybe? "It was nice talking to you!"

I watched them dance. They looked so good together. I could see why he was with a girl like Tina and why a girl like Tina was with him. They just worked. They come from the same world. Guys like Rusty don't dance like that with girls like me.

I spotted Andy leaning against the wall with his arms crossed. He was staring at me for some reason. I looked away for a minute and when I looked again, he was still staring. He was starting to creep me out, so I made my excuses to Darryl about having a headache and left the social early.

The next morning, I went for a shower before the other girls got up. I put my towel just outside the cubicle and when I went to grab it, it wasn't there. I checked the floor to see if it had fallen off the hook, but no. Someone had taken it—along with my clothes that I'd left by the sink.

I yelled out, "This isn't funny!" Some of the kids were playing a prank on me. Or so I thought. I had no choice. I couldn't wait in there all day. I had to cover myself with my hands and take a step outside. And as soon as I did, a bright flash hit my eyes. I jumped back and screamed!

Then I heard those familiar laughs...

Tina was the one who took the picture. The polaroid fell to the ground, and she bent down to pick it up, shaking it while it developed. More laughter.

"Well, this will make an interesting addition to the memories wall in the mess hall," she said.

I'd already covered myself back up. I could see my t-shirt and shorts in Nancy's hand. "You wouldn't dare," I said, trying to hold back the tears. It was too late. "I'll go straight to Darryl!"

That wiped the smile off her face. But her eyes became cold. She passed the camera to Lydia and walked right up to me, so we were face-to-face. I won't lie, I was scared of her in that moment.

"Do you really think I'm scared of some pothead?" Her hot morning breath hit my face like garlic. Not so perfect after all. She carried on before I could answer. "But I'm a nice person. I'm gonna make you a little deal."

"What sort of deal?" I asked.

Tina turned around and Nancy threw my clothes over to her. "I'll give your clothes back and I'll burn that photo if you do as I say from now on." Her evil grin returned. "If I tell you to sit at the end of the table, you do it. If I tell you to fetch my food, you do it." She paused and leaned in closer. "And if I tell you to never flirt with Rusty again—well, you finish the sentence."

"I wasn't—" I began, but there was no use arguing. I wanted to rip every strand of hair out of her head. "I do it," I whispered.

"You got it." Tina shoved my clothes into my chest and started to walk away.

"Wait—the photo!"

She looked at Nancy and Lydia individually, fanning herself with the polaroid. "I'm gonna hold onto this for insurance. Just until I'm satisfied that you're holding up your end of the deal, I'm a fair girl like that."

The girls walked away. It took me a second to get over the shock of what just happened, but I hurried back inside the shower block and got dressed, trying to wipe away the tears.

She's evil. Tina is pure evil!

Why is she doing this to me?

Last night we had our 4th of July celebration. Darryl arranged a firework display for the kids which kept them entertained for the evening. He also got us a couple of packs of beer and invited the counselors to have a quiet gathering by the fire once the kids were in bed. I'd never tried alcohol before—not even at a wedding—but I didn't know what all the fuss was about. Beer is disgusting! Still, I drank a few.

Rusty brought his cassette player with him so we could listen to some music (**REMINDER:** buy the *Footloose* soundtrack when you get home) and offered me his sweater because I was rubbing my arms. I spotted Tina staring at me, so I just shook my head.

"Here," he said, stripping out of it. "It's freezing."

He held the sweater out for me, but I pushed it away. "I'm fine, honestly."

"Okay, well I'm gonna leave it here," he said, resting it on the log I was sitting on, "and you can put it on if you change your mind."

I wanted to say thank you, but I could feel Tina's eyes burning into me. I just put my head down and waited for him to sit back down. When he did, he looked so confused. Hurt even. I felt so rude.

When we were all sat down, Darryl cheers'd us and thanked us for our hard work so far. He even pulled out a joint for us to pass round. I refused to take a hit and so did Andy.

"How did you end up running this place, Darryl?" Rusty asked after taking a toke.

"My parents own it," he began. "They ran the place for twenty years, but they decided to close it down back in 1980."

Most of the other counselors stayed silent. They looked on while Darryl took a long swig of beer, waiting for the next part of the story. When it didn't come, Tina was the first to speak up. Obviously.

"Why did they do that?" she asked.

Darryl laughed. "It's getting pretty late and I'm sure you all don't want a horror story before bed."

Tina wasn't happy to leave it there. "I love horror stories."

"Tina, come on," Rusty said. "It's none of our business."

Darryl sighed while Rusty passed him what was left of the joint. "Are you sure you wanna hear this?"

Everyone nodded except for Rusty and Andy.

Darryl took one last toke and threw the rest of the joint into the fire. It sparked and crackled in the flames. "For years Camp Stanleyside had a good reputation. All the kids loved it here, the counselors were never any trouble and any accidents that did happen were never severe. In 1980 it changed. Turn of the decade, as my dad would say.

"One night, two counselors went out into the woods alone." Darryl pointed. "Just by the lake there. The next day when everyone realized they were missing, my dad and two other counselors went out into the woods to look for them. All they found was a shoe and some blood. The police came to investigate and suggested they close the camp for the rest of the summer. The parents of the boys would see to it anyway, but my parents refused. The kids' parents paid good money for them to come here—better than what they pay now, by the way—and they couldn't afford to take the hit.

While the police investigated, my parents reassured the kids and the other counselors that everything was fine. Business as usual. Of course, the counselors weren't satisfied with that and some of them threatened to quit. They couldn't really afford it, but my parents paid them extra if they carried on and kept quiet. Dad even drafted up a fake NDA to make sure. He was always business-minded, and he couldn't have anyone tarnishing the camp's name with a potential murder case."

Darryl stopped to take a drink. Nancy and Lydia looked at each other and I'd be lying if I said it didn't make me happy to see them both look so scared. However, the story spooked me too.

Tina rolled her eyes. "Oh, *BULL. SHIT.* I've heard the kids tell scarier stories! And do you really expect us to believe your dad would cover up all these deaths? Get real!"

"Tina!" Rusty turned off the cassette player. Suddenly he was interested. "Did they ever find the bodies?"

"There's more," Darryl said. "Those two boys, they weren't the only deaths that year."

Another eyeroll from Tina.

I gulped hard, trying not to believe what I was hearing. But the truth has a funny ring to it.

"A couple of weeks later, everything was fine. It was like the other counselors had forgotten about the whole thing and just carried on, at least that's what Dad said. It was getting towards the end of the season and although the police found nothing, my dad banned anyone from going into the woods—even during the day.

"This time it was a girl and a boy. They snuck out one night, said they were going to the lake. That's what the other kids said anyway. The next morning the whole camp searched for them. The woods, the lake, the perimeters—nothing. Not a trace. Finally, my parents had to pull the plug and they shut the camp down before the season was out. Of course, they got the blame and were slapped with lawsuits from all the parents. The legal fees alone cost them more than the camp was worth—"

"Okay. Now I know you're lying," Tina interrupted. "If that really happened, why are you running the camp now?"

Darryl looked her dead in the eyes. "I inherited it when my parents died in a car accident three years ago."

"Shit, Darryl," Rusty said. "I'm sorry."

I didn't know if it was the chill in the air or how the story made me feel, but I couldn't stop shaking. I felt like there was someone or something watching me.

 I had to ask: "What do you think happened to them, Darryl?"

Darryl stared into the fire for a moment before he looked at me. He burst into laughter.

"Oh man, you should have seen the looks on your faces!"

Rusty shook his head and joined in. "You had me there for a second."

Tina sighed. "I knew it."

I couldn't laugh though. I was still shaking. I finally gave in and turned to grab Rusty's sweater when I felt something smooth on top of it. I jumped off the log, nearly falling into the fire as I did and screamed.

"What?" Rusty said. "What is it?"

"There's a snake on your sweater!"

While most of the other counselors laughed, especially Tina, Rusty

62

came over and picked up the snake. "It's okay," he said. "It's just a little fella. He's harmless."

Rusty took the snake over to the grass and let it go.

"I think that's enough scares for one night," Darryl said. "Time for bed."

But I couldn't sleep at all. I was shaking all the way through the night.

CHAPTER III

THE FIRST DAY

Being woken up by the sound of a loud horn wasn't the best start to the morning. His cabin buddies didn't have much to say when they woke up, besides "Good morning". Luke headed straight for the shower and the others followed not long after. As Brody got dressed, he couldn't stop thinking about what he had read in the notebook the night before. Four kids went missing in this place and nobody knew what happened to them.

As if this place couldn't get any more fucking weird, he thought.

While he had the chance, he took the notebook out of his drawer to read on. A couple of entries about Tina being a bitch, *no surprise there*, Marla still being a little brat, and Rusty. It was like reading a cringeworthy John Hughes movie at times, but he'd take his entertainment where he could get it. More importantly, he wanted to know anything and everything he could about Camp Silver Oaks, or Camp Stanleyside, as it used to be called. His reading session was interrupted by Josh who came into the cabin with spikes of wet hair stuck to his forehead. He looked older without his glasses. Less child-like.

"What'cha reading there?" he asked, squinting. The nosy little shit probably couldn't see.

Brody put the notebook back into his drawer. "Just something Bart gave me."

It was the only thing that came into his head. It seemed like a believable lie. Of course, he could tell them the truth, that he found it in a box by the lake. But first he wanted to figure out *why* a diary from the 1980s was hidden away.

Josh put his glasses on. "Oh, cool. He never gave anything to me when I arrived here. What is it?"

Before Brody could tell Josh to mind his own business, Pete and Akeeb came through the door.

"Seriously, dude, everyone does it!" Pete said to Akeeb, who was shaking his head.

"No, *dude*, they do not. It's disgusting!" Akeeb nodded over to Brody. "Do you pee in the shower, Brody? Or do you use a toilet? *Like everybody else.*"

"Erm—"

"See!" Akeeb said.

Pete wasn't having any of it. "Well, it saves time!"

While Josh stood in the middle of the room, frowning at both Pete and Akeeb hashing out where they urinate, Brody thought it was the perfect time to make his exit. Rich came through the door next and offered a shy smile at Brody, but he wouldn't look him in the eyes.

"Wait, Brody!" Josh said. "We'll come with you."

Brody sighed. "Awesome."

*

Luke was sitting at a table waiting for them when they walked into the mess hall. He was already eating his breakfast. Brody saw an empty spot in the corner of the room and headed straight for it.

"Wait—" Akeeb said. "You're gonna sit with us, right?"

Brody looked back at the small table with only one chair. It seemed more appealing than sitting with Luke and his posse, but when all five of them stared, waiting for his response, he cracked under the pressure. "Yeah, sure," he said, quickly changing his direction to the serving station. "I'm starved. I'm gonna get some food."

There was a small line for the food. Burnt pancakes and bacon. There certainly seemed to be a pattern with how the food was served at Silver Oaks so far, which was why Brody let out a sigh of relief when he spotted the box of Corn Flakes. While he waited in line, he couldn't help but overhear the two girls in front of him, whispering to one another.

"It's someone from Cabin 4," the blonde girl with a southern drawl said. "None of them have come in for breakfast yet."

The ginger girl nodded. "I'll bet you my last pack of Oreos that it's Jessica."

"Do you think she was—" the blonde girl stopped. She spun her head round, spotting Brody and shifted her eyes at her red-headed, freckled friend for a moment before she forced a smile. "Oh, hi! You're the new guy, aren't you?"

"Brody," he said, which made the blonde narrow her eyes.

"Cynthia Callington-Rowley," she said extending her hand like she was royalty. Cynthia probably thought she was too, judging by the way she straightened her back as she did so.

Brody kept his hands at his sides. "Nice name."

Cynthia's eyes narrowed even more, to the point where they looked closed.

"Well, it's nice to meet you, Brody." Cynthia remembered her friend was standing next to her, placing a gentle hand on her back. The ginger girl gave Brody a small wave and a weak toothy smile. "This is Allie. We're from Cabin 6. You're in Cabin 12 with Luke and the boys, aren't you?"

"Unfortunately," Brody mumbled.

"Pardon?"

"Yes, I am."

"Lucky you." Cynthia looked him up and down. "I'm sure Luke will be a fine example to you. Now, I don't want to be rude, but we are holding up the line here, so if you'll excuse me."

Cynthia grabbed Allie by the arm. She batted her eyelashes at Brody before Cynthia moved her forward. The whispers continued. He guessed their topic of conversation had changed to him when he overheard her say "Asshole."

So much for that southern charm.

The atmosphere in the mess hall was quiet, a far contrast from the night before at dinner. Campers pushed their food around with glum faces, talking quietly, if at all.

Josh didn't read the room. He started grilling Brody about his interests and his life, as though he was on *The Late Show*. He continued the grilling—loudly—through breakfast.

"What was your favorite class at school?" he asked, going on to answer the question himself. "Mine was drama, I've always loved the theater. Do you like the theater?"

Brody tried to stay polite, but he had lost interest after the first question. "Not really. Erm, art, I guess."

"We have an amazing art class here! Don't we, Luke?"

Luke tapped his fingers on the table, looking past Josh. "I think Uncle John's about to say something," he said, changing the subject.

Sure enough, Uncle John got up from the table of counselors and stood in front of the serving station with his hands together. The whole room shuffled in their seats and gave him their full attention. He waited patiently with a curve of the mouth until everyone was settled.

"Good morning, campers," he began, "I'm going to address something I'm sure a lot of you will already know." For a moment, Uncle John let the thought sink in and looked around at the varied reactions of his prisoners. A few side-eyed glances, raised eyebrows, the occasional shrug. Satisfied, he continued. "Last night, Jessica Bowden sadly left us. She was caught trying to escape the grounds during the heavy rainfall and had to be dealt with accordingly."

Dealt with accordingly? Brody had no idea who the girl was, but the incident seemed to shake up the whole camp. Maybe Luke was telling the truth after all about the so-called siren the night before. Brody looked over to Luke, who was glaring at him. Almost as if he were reading Brody's mind.

"*Pay attention!*" Luke mouthed.

Brody rolled his eyes. Such a kiss-ass.

"We will all miss Jessica," Uncle John continued, "but please, don't let her foolishness dampen your spirits today. It's a beautiful day, so let's embrace the weather and feel joy, express laughter and enjoy the hot sun."

Brody leaned into Josh's ear. "Is this guy for-fucking-real or what?" he whispered.

All Brody received back was a scowl and pursed lips. Josh shuffled away from Brody and listened to Uncle John like he was performing a sermon in church. That's how most of them looked at him—like some sort of idol. Straight backs, leaning forward to catch his every word. Brody didn't get it. He was just some dude in a button-down shirt.

"Well said, Uncle John!" Luke yelled, banging his cutlery on the table.

Everyone else followed his lead while Uncle John flapped

his hands at them, bashful from the admiration. He finished the assembly with a quick bow of his head and sat back down with the rest of the counselors. In the space of seconds, the feeling of the room changed and the volume of chatter, laughter—and eating—increased. Next to Uncle John, Bart sat looking at Brody. He gave him a cautious smile.

*

After breakfast, one of the counselors dropped off a plan of the activities for the week to Brody. He would be taking an art class that was going to be led by Pamela, the counselor. Outside, her group had assembled in a huddle. A mixture of genders.

"Don't let that chirpy face fool you," a girl said behind him, nodding toward Pamela. "She's a total bitch and, in all honesty, a bit of a psycho."

The girl was shorter than him, with a black bob haircut that she had probably cut herself judging by how uneven it was. He also noticed the two gaping holes in her ears where plugs used to be. She grinned at Brody, and he found her smile infectious. She also seemed like the first *real* person he had met so far.

"Yeah, I've already met her," Brody said. "She's also got a lot of strength in her for a girl her size."

"What—so short girls can't be strong? Oh, you're one of *those* boys?" The girl teased, cocking her eyebrow. "You sexist pig."

Brody loved her already. "I'm Bro—"

"Brody Jackson," she interrupted. "Yes, I know. You're the new boy, everybody knows your name. You're the new shiny toy around here until the next one comes along. Blah, blah, blah. I'm Daphne—and yes—I was named after a cartoon character."

He thought of Bart and started laughing. He couldn't help it. His snorts prompted another raised eyebrow from Daphne. "You're not the only one, I think," he giggled. "Bart?"

"Ah, of course."

Pamela lifted her chin over at Brody and Daphne, signaling them to join the group of campers huddled in front of her. Once everyone was present, she handed out a stack of notebooks. Brody looked around at the battered pads, some decorated with doodles and patterns, while his was fresh with just his name written on it.

"I'm sure I don't need to introduce Brody to all of you, as I'm sure you're aware of him by now," Pamela said, as though his very existence was an inconvenience to her. "We're going to start fresh this week with a new project, so we're all doing the same thing."

Daphne sighed. "I swear to god, if it's writing down texture words again, I'm gonna go insane."

"Now I was thinking that perhaps we could start with textures," Pamela said with a grin.

"Oh! There it is. God, she's so predictable," Daphne said through gritted teeth. "She does this every time someone new comes to the class."

"I'm sorry for spoiling your artistic vison," Brody said, flicking through his blank notebook. "Shouldn't we have, like, sketch pads? These are a little small. This is an art class, right?"

"This is to write down your ideas, your words, your mood, your emotions," she exaggerated the words with false enthusiasm, like an art curator looking at a red dot. "What feelings do the trees bring out in you? How does the wind feel on your skin? C'mon, use your imagination, Jackson. Also, it's probably so they can read them after and see what we're thinking or something."

"Oh, perfect. I'll give them something fun to read."

"I'd keep it clean if I were you." Daphne's grin vanished. "Seriously."

Once their assignment was decided, Pamela instructed the group to explore the camp for an hour and write down some words. It was like being on a field trip, only this was Brody's home now, so it didn't quite have the same effect.

"Come on," Daphne said, tugging him by his t-shirt. "I know somewhere we can get the best inspiration."

Daphne led the way to the archery range on the field opposite the mess hall. There were some trees around, but nothing of major interest. Without a word, Daphne sat on the field and Brody followed. He spotted Luke in the class, demonstrating some impressive skills with the bow. *Such a show-off.* The class was being observed by Bart, who gave them a wave across the field. Daphne did the waving for them both.

"Told you it was a good view," she said. "What's your poison?"

"Well, I've always been fond of vodka."

"No," she smirked. "I mean do you like girls or boys?"

Brody wasn't surprised at her frankness. "I'll tell if you do."

"Both," Daphne shrugged, taking out a piece of paper that she tucked into the waistband of her shorts. She unfolded it and smoothed it over a page littered with words that went over the ruled lines. It was an anime-style picture of a girl dressed in the Camp Silver Oaks uniform. "Her name's Cynthia. She's the blonde girl on the end."

"Yes, I've already been acquainted with Lady Callington-Rowley."

He could see the attraction, Cynthia looked like the athletic type. She was probably homecoming queen and captain of the girls' soccer team before she came to Camp Silver Oaks. He couldn't imagine what it was that she could have done to end up in a place like this.

Luke shot an arrow into the target in front of him, not too far off the center. Cynthia went next, pulling back her bow with little hesitation.

Bullseye.

"What's the deal with Luke?" Brody asked Daphne, while she continued to work on her sketch of Cynthia. "He seems like a bit of a dick."

"Well, he's just absorbed by this place. Almost everyone is, haven't you noticed?"

Brody nodded. "What about you?"

"I just keep my head down, mind my own business, and play along. I'll be out of here in a few months. Besides, Uncle John sees all."

Daphne came at Brody with her hands cramped up, making some ghoulish noise. It made her look more goofy than scary.

"And what's Uncle John's deal?"

"The less you know about Uncle John, the better. And that's about as much as I know about him." Daphne looked ahead at the range, and quickly changed the subject. "I think he has the hots for you, you know."

Brody scoffed. "Who, Luke? It wouldn't surprise me."

"No, Bart."

Instead of focusing on the former criminals who had actual weapons in their hands, Bart's attention was fixed on Brody. "Well, he's certainly there everywhere I turn, that's for sure."

"Bart's one of the good ones, you know. He really is a sweet guy."

"Hmm, with a dark side I bet."

Daphne stopped sketching. "Haven't we all got one of those? That's why we're here."

Brody nodded.

"You never did say what your poison is," Daphne said, after a few moments.

"A gentleman never kisses and tells," Brody said, grinning.

"Gay. I knew it."

Brody shrugged. "Sorry to disappoint."

"Don't flatter yourself, Jackson."

*

The art class was a dud. Once the hour was up, Pamela blew a whistle for them to come back over to her and they made their way into the arts building. The most Brody decided to write down was *green, crunchy,* and *wood,* mostly so Pamela wouldn't read what he was thinking. For the rest of the class he ended up sketching the old train tracks by his house, under a night's sky. He'd often sit on a tree near them back home. He wished he was still there, listening to *The Killing Moon* on repeat in the dark. It sounded grim, but it was his happy place. Somewhere he could get away from everything, and everyone, and just let the music take him. He was trying to figure out how to do that at Silver Oaks. Even when he took a dump, he could feel eyes on him. Watching.

The class cleared out of the arts building once Pamela told them it was over. Daphne gave him a quick wave and shot out of there as quick as she could.

"Brody?" Pamela said, using her finger to call him forward like a dog.

"Yes."

"Would you mind putting away the supplies and the pads over there?" she pointed at the drawers behind her. "Second drawer for the pads, please. I have a counselors meeting."

"Erm, don't you need to, like, lock up or something?"

Pamela narrowed her eyes but kept her sickly smile. "Well, if something goes missing, I'll know who it was, won't I?"

What did she think he was gonna do? Steal a few paint brushes?

"Sure, no problem," Brody said. "Have fun at your meeting."

Pamela kept her eyes on him until she was out the door.

Such a fucking weirdo.

*

After dinner, someone knocked on the cabin door, where Brody was alone. He was laying on the bed, just about to continue reading some more entries from the notebook, which he quickly stashed under his pillow.

They entered without announcing themselves.

Brody frowned. "Dude, I could have been naked or something!"

"All alone tonight?" Bart asked, ignoring the statement, and poking his head around the door.

"Yeah, some of the boys are gonna go and sit round the campfire or something."

"I know, I was just with them. There's a big group of us, actually. You should come and join."

"Nah."

Bart put his hands on his hips. "What? You don't want to hear my awesome rendition of a Tears for Fears song on the acoustic? Boy, you are missing out!"

Brody couldn't help but laugh at the thought. "Yeah, I'll pass."

"Come on, I'd love to have you there."

"Why?"

Bart approached and sat tentatively on the end of Brody's bed. "What if I said it's because I think you're just about the only person that seems to laugh *with* me, rather than *at* me."

"Oh no, it's definitely *at* you."

"Ah okay, but still."

There was a shyness to Bart in that moment, one that Brody didn't expect from someone so happy-go-lucky as him. He wondered how much of that was a front.

Brody leaned forward. "Look, *if* I come, it's only so you'll leave me alone and stop trying to sell me these extra-curricular activities every time I take a breath. Deal?"

Bobbing his head from side-to-side, Bart eventually shrugged.

"I can't ask fairer than that, I guess," he said. Then his eyes popped out of his head. "Wait—does that mean you're coming?"

Bart leaped off the bed like an excited puppy. His mouth wide open.

"What...is going on?" Brody said, cringing inside.

Bart cupped his hands over his mouth. "Campers, important announcement!" he shouted into the air. "Brody Jackson is coming to the campfire!"

"Oh my god!" Brody covered his face to hide the laughter. "Please stop or I'll change my mind."

Bart composed himself. "Sorry, sorry. I'm just happy you're coming."

"Clearly!" Brody smirked at him in a way that made Bart's shyness return. He smiled down at his feet. "Just give me about half an hour and I'll be out."

"No problem," Bart said and made his way over to the door.

"Bart?" Brody called out as he opened the door.

"Yeah?"

"Which Tears for Fears song?"

"*Head Over Heels*, of course."

"My favorite." Brody smiled. "I can't wait to hear it."

Bart smiled back and closed the door behind him. As soon as he did, Brody dug the notebook out from underneath his pillow.

Yesterday I got stuck with Andy teaching the kids how to build rafts. It was meant to be Tina on the roster, but Darryl said she was sick and couldn't do it.

Sick, my ass! She looked perfectly fine the night before when she was sitting on Rusty's knee, with her mouth sucking his face every two seconds. I guess they really are into each other now. They were never like that at first. I've done my best to avoid Rusty at all costs since Tina threatened to show everyone that picture.

And Tina. The **BITCH**!

Mostly she just looks right through me whenever we bump into one another. I thought the silent treatment I received in this place couldn't get any worse and then I was lumbered with Andy. But to my surprise, with the kids, he was a regular chatterbox. It was just with the rest of the counselors that he didn't speak so much. It was like being around a completely different person.

The heat from the early morning sun made the air feel sticky. Inside the woods, despite the decent amount of shade, it was near unbearable. We assigned the kids to start looking for large pieces of wood to build their rafts with. Instead of walking with the campers, Andy decided to walk with me.

"Hot?" he said, after a few minutes.

When I looked at him, shocked by the fact he *actually* spoke to me, he was smiling. Despite his whole dark and moody appearance, it was a warm smile. "Erm, yeah," I said. "You?"

Andy shrugged. "Maybe it wasn't the best day to wear black, but I left my preppy clothes at home."

"Oh, I'm sorry."

"I was joking."

I felt like an idiot, especially when he started laughing. "Oh, I—" I looked down at the t-shirt he was wearing. Black, of course, with red lettering. It read: **The Sisters of Mercy**. Maybe he went to a catholic school or something? "I like your shirt."

Andy frowned at me. "Thanks, I like yours too."

I was wearing my bright pink t-shirt with a kitten on it, so I knew he was being sarcastic. I thought that was the end of our exchange, the silence returned for a while until he stopped.

"I just wanted to say, don't let Tina get to you," he said. "That Rusty guy isn't worth it."

I didn't know where to look. "Excuse me?"

"I may not talk a lot. Mostly because I think the majority of the counselors are dicks—present company excluded—but I see everything." He smiled again.

I was back to feeling uncomfortable around him. And I was mad. Spying on me and the other counselors? What a creep! How much had he seen exactly?

"I think we should call the kids back over," I said, storming ahead.

It was awkward, just as I imagined it would be, for the rest of the class. I suggested splitting the kids into two groups so we could help them put their rafts together. Every now and then I would spot Andy looking over at me. I just ignored it. I wanted to get the class over with as quickly as possible, so I did a lot of the raft building myself. My team was so slow.

Once the raft was built, I made sure the ropes were tight enough and the wood was sturdy enough to support us. Including me, there were five. Andy's team were done too, and we pushed the rafts out on opposite sides of the dock. Even though it was far too hot, and I was doing most of the rowing, the lake looked so beautiful under the sun.

The other raft was well ahead of us after a while. Clearly, Andy had the stronger team. Most of the kids on mine started to moan that their arms were getting tired and that they were hungry. I stopped the rowing and called out to Andy to turn around, but he didn't hear me. He was too far away. I told the kids to shuffle round on the raft and we'd make our way back to camp.

The water started to sway when we moved around, and the raft started to rock with it. I put it down to the weight distribution and it stopped once we were settled. But as we rowed back over to the dock, it happened again.

A huge bump under the raft.

It made me drop the stick I was using as an oar, and I grabbed onto a piece of wood for support. The kids looked at me and started laughing. Of course they did.

It happened again. Only this time, it turned the raft over.

I went under. There was a strong force in the water that pulled me down, like a strong tide at the beach. If it wasn't for the fact that I struggled to gain control from the impact of falling in, I would have found the water oddly refreshing. But I was afraid. I couldn't see a thing down there. I kicked my legs as much as I could and managed to swim up, back to the light above. I resurfaced from the water and one-by-one the other kids did too. Except for Tony.

I called out his name and the kids started to panic. I looked behind me at the other raft. Andy dived into the water and swam towards us. I swam under the surface again to try and look for him. All I could see was a murky green haze. Nothing but dirty water.

I came back up and there was still no sign of him. Andy was getting closer. I screamed his name and the kids started to cry. A child had drowned, and it was my fault. It was on my watch. What would I say to his parents? How would I live with something like that? The tears came flooding out of my eyes.

And then, further from the rest of us, Tony finally came to the surface. He was coughing and frantically flapping.

"Thank god!" I swam to him.

As I did, I noticed the pieces of split wood in the water. The raft hadn't just come apart, it was broken.

Andy and I took Tony to the infirmary inside Darryl's office. He was fine, just a little sick from consuming some of the water, but he would live. Suzanne, the nurse, gave him the once-over and asked him what happened. But he just shrugged, said he fell in.

Darryl made me and Andy stay behind.

"What the hell happened?" Darryl's eyes bulged out of their sockets. It was the first time I'd ever seen him look so concerned—or serious.

"The raft just...went over," I said, avoiding his gaze. "It was like something hit it."

"Christ, this is all I need." Darryl paced the room, massaging his head. "That kid could have drowned! Did you make sure the raft was secure before you went out?"

"Of course, I did! I mean, it had come apart and the wood was broken but—"

Darryl slammed his first on his desk. "Then it wasn't secure, was it?"

"Look, Darryl," Andy said. "I watched her put that thing together. It was as tight as it could be. Trust me."

After a few more paces, Darryl looked to the ceiling and bit his lip. "Okay," he eventually said. "Okay. It happened and it won't happen again. No more raft building for the rest of the summer. Easy."

Even if Darryl asked me to do it again, I would refuse. There was no way I would put myself in that position again. But Andy looked disheartened.

After Darryl dismissed us from his office, I walked ahead of Andy. I just wanted to get a shower and into some fresh clothes.

"Hey! Wait up," he said, running after me. "Are you okay?"

"No, I'm not."

I tried to speed up, but Andy got in front of me. "Talk to me."

After weeks of not saying a word to me, suddenly he wanted to talk. I started to doubt myself. Did I really make sure the raft was secure enough? "I just don't understand it," I said. "Did you see what happened?"

Andy shook his head. "I turned around and saw you were gone. Then I saw you all come up to the surface. I figured you all just fell in, but..."

"But what?"

"The raft. It wasn't there. It had come apart."

I squinted at him. "So, all that stuff you said back there was bullshit? You're saying it's my fault?"

"No, that's not what I'm saying." Andy shook his head again. "You said something hit the raft, right?"

"Yes, it did."

"Hard enough to split it?"

"Well, you saw the raft after it happened."

Andy looked down at his feet for a moment. "What could have done that?"

I didn't know what else to say. "A gator, maybe?"

"There are no gators around here. If there were we wouldn't be letting kids into that lake."

Andy was right, it was stupid. Maybe it was my fault, after all. But one thing's for sure. I won't be going near or into that lake anytime soon.

So, the word got out about the incident at the lake.

Tina made a point of bringing it up at lunch yesterday in front of the other counselors. Nancy and Lydia laughed, of course. I sat at the end of the table, there were two spaces between me and Andy. We hadn't talked since that day, and I went back to avoiding him.

"Seriously, even I could put a raft together properly," Tina said, acting like I wasn't even there. Rusty sat next to her, digging into his potato salad. He didn't seem to care that she was making fun of me anymore. "I mean, poor Tony! He could have died. Any of those kids could have. So neglectful!"

"Darryl should fire her ass," Nancy said.

Lydia nodded. "I agree."

"This never would have happened if I was there," Tina said.

Andy dropped his fork. The clatter against his plate made everyone look his way, and he stared directly at Tina. "And yet, you weren't there, were you? And even if you were, you probably would have just spent your time staring into that little mirror you carry around. Because the only person you care about is yourself, Tina."

Nobody said anything. Even Tina was stuck for words. Hell, even I was!

"Accidents happen," Andy continued. "So, for once in your miserable life, shut the hell up."

Tina spun round to Rusty. "Are you gonna let that little *freak* speak to me like that?"

Rusty shrugged. He didn't know what to say at first. "Look man, there's no need to be mean."

"Well, *man*, if you want to talk about being mean, just look at your girl there." Andy turned to me and winked. I couldn't help it, the fact he stood up to Tina like that made me grin ear-to-ear.

Tina stood and as usual Nancy and Lydia followed suit. "Thanks for having my back, Rusty!" she said. Before she stormed off, she looked over at me. Eyes like darts. "This isn't over."

Rusty sighed and ran after Tina. Andy picked up his fork and carried on eating.

"Well said," Rikki, another camp counselor said.

Andy didn't respond.

CHAPTER IV

A CAMPFIRE STORY

Brody jumped when the cabin door opened.

"Jesus, Bart!" he said, hiding the notebook back under his pillow for the second time that night. "You scared the living shit out of me!"

Bart frowned. "You said you'd be half an hour. I've told everyone you're coming now, so you can't let me down."

Brody didn't know what time it was, he was deep into reading the diary entries and lost track of time. "I would never want to do that," he said, rolling his eyes. "Lead the way, Simpson!"

"You missed my opening number, you know."

"What a shame…"

*

Not far from the main field and the archery range, there was a set-up for the campfire that included some old logs circled around the center. Brody followed Bart to the fire, dragging his feet behind him like a reluctant teenager. The flames looked as though they towered into the misty-blue skyline, and the ashes flickered into the air. There was a view of the lake from the campfire, but it was too dark to see the water from where the fire lit the sky. He sat down next to Rich who had barely spoke a word to him since he arrived. Most of the campers who hadn't introduced themselves to him yet stared at him like he was an extra-terrestrial.

Several of them waved. "Hi Brody", "Hey Brody", "Wassup Brody!"

God, this phony bullshit is getting tiresome. And it was only day two.

Daphne waved from across the flames. She sat next to Cynthia who was rubbing her elbows and wearing a sweatshirt and a hooded jacket, even though it wasn't cold. Daphne shifted her eyes from Brody to Cynthia and gave a secretive, goofy smile. Like he didn't already know that she was thrilled to be sat next to her.

"I picked up a stray," Bart said to the group, winking at me. "I'm sure most of you know Brody by now."

Mortified at the attention, Brody looked down and kicked some of the dirt between his shoes while everyone said, "Hi". When he looked up, Daphne was smirking at him.

"So, are we ready for another song?" Bart asked, picking up his acoustic which had a sticker with a peace sign on it. Of course it did. He rested the guitar on his knee, thinking of something to play.

Cynthia raised her hand like she was in a classroom. Bart nodded for her to speak. "As much as we all love listening to your voice—" and she said this with a clear indication that she didn't "—I think we could do with a good campfire story tonight."

Bart's face became a mixture of surprise and sadness. Brody felt bad for him, he obviously wanted to rock out some old songs on his guitar that none of them had heard.

"I mean…we can…sure," Bart cleared his throat, laying the guitar to one side and looking a little wounded. "But nothing too over the top, okay?"

At first, Brody didn't understand why everyone was so excited to hear some dumb story. Then it occurred to him that he hadn't seen any televisions or even that many books in Camp Silver Oaks at all. The campers were starved of entertainment, and this was their way to get it.

"Rich, why don't you tell us the one about The Night Flyer," Cynthia suggested.

Rich didn't look up when Cynthia addressed him. His knees started to shake, and the log trembled under Brody from the impact. While everyone waited eagerly for his response, staring at him, it became clear it was making Rich anxious. Bart saw it, too, and intervened.

"Oh no, Cynthia. We'll all have nightmares!" he said. "Why don't we have something a little less scary?"

Cynthia stared off into the lake, and then snapped back to lock eyes with Brody. "Do *you* have any stories you want to share?"

"Not really, no," he said with a shrug. "I'm not much of a storyteller."

"Just use your imagination. You're at camp, it's nighttime. Go from there."

Brody was about to resist once again but rolled his eyes and nodded. "Okay, fine. But I doubt it'll be any good."

Everyone got themselves comfortable and waited for him to start. Brody stared up at the sky for a moment, but he had the perfect inspiration.

"It was a hot summer's night in 1980. The camp was called—Camp—erm—Shallow Lake," he begun and already felt like an idiot when some of them laughed. "The counselors were having a party in one of their cabins, and they thought the kids were tucked away in bed, asleep. But—erm—Jimmy—

had other ideas...can I stop now? This is just painful."

Bart nodded. "Of course, we can just play some songs instead."

God, he really is desperate to perform, Brody thought.

Cynthia wasn't done. "Oh, come on, Brody"

"Okay, fine. So, Jimmy," Brody continued, "and another counselor called Tyler snuck away from the party. Drunk on the hot night and cheap vodka, Jimmy suggested that they went into the woods to make-out—and—erm—other stuff. So, there they were. Alone, sucking each other's—"

"That's enough," Bart interrupted. "That's more than enough."

Brody grinned. "I was going to say *faces*."

"Fine. Just keep it clean."

"And then they heard a noise. A twig snapping. They looked around, but nobody was there. Suddenly Jimmy wasn't in the mood and suggested they leave, but Tyler still wanted some of that sweet summer lovin'." Brody bounced his eyebrows up and down with a smirk. "They went back to sucking faces and another twig snapped. Closer now. Jimmy stormed off, said, 'Fu—', *sorry*, 'Screw this, I'm out of here!'

"Jimmy was halfway back to camp when he heard Tyler's screams in the distance. He was so close to safety, but his boyfriend was in trouble. So, he decided to go back..."

Despite his amateur storytelling, the other campers leaned in. They were engaged. Cynthia especially. "And then what?" she asked, eyes wide behind the flames.

"Nobody ever heard or saw them again—"

The end of Brody's story was interrupted by a chorus of boos from some of the campers.

Brody shrugged. "What?"

"Come on, Jackson!" Daphne said. "You can do better than that."

Cynthia nodded. "I agree, Darla."

"It's Daphne," she responded. It must've been like taking a bullet.

Bart slapped his knees. "How about that song?"

"Well, that's what happened," Brody said, ignoring Bart, just like everyone else had. He hesitated for a minute, but if they wanted a campfire story, he would give them one. "It's a true story."

Cynthia laughed, clapping her hands together. "Of course it is, darling. Aren't they all?"

"No, this *actually* happened. It happened here, in fact," Brody said. "At Camp Silver Oaks."

Silence.

Rich's leg was working overtime. If he shook it any faster, he would have dug a hole in the ground. Daphne looked down at her feet while Cynthia narrowed her eyes at Brody. Even though the campfire story he read about turned out to be fiction, he was going to take a leaf out of Darryl's book and fuck with these campers.

"Oh, really? And how would you know that *new boy*?" she asked.

Brody wasn't about to reveal his source, and he wasn't about to be embarrassed by some spoilt princess. "Well, I know that Silver Oaks used to be called Camp Stanleyside back in the 1980s. And those two boys—"

"Jimmy and Tyler?" Cynthia interrupted.

"I don't know their real names, but they disappeared and all they found was a bloody shoe," Brody nodded toward the trees, "out there in the woods. Then two *more* kids went missing a few weeks later. They closed the camp down until 1984—"

It was Bart who interrupted Brody this time. "Okay, we're done with this story, Brody." His voice was sharp. "Thank you."

"But I was just getting to the good part!" Brody pretended to sulk, but Bart wasn't amused.

"Let's call it a night, guys." Bart said.

"Well, that was a letdown." Cynthia shook her head. "That's what keeps you up at night? A childish urban legend told at *every* camp ever?"

He didn't know if it was what she said, how she said it, or the fact she prodded for it, but Brody's cheeks burned hotter than the campfire. "Okay, you want to know what keeps me up at night? I'll start with how I was plucked from my home and sent to a camp full of people who can't do anything but be polite and smile and act fake-as-fuck. Is that a good start? Or should I tell you about how my own mother couldn't look at me during my conviction, or how my father hasn't spoken directly to me in over four years? Oh, and let's not forget how I set fire to my school. Or may—"

"Brody, that's enough now…"

Uncle John appeared from the shadows. His face glowed by the orange flames of the campfire. The light brought out harsh lines on his skin, which were hard to see in daylight, and aged him considerably by at least ten years. More than anything, the fire brought out a yellowish hue in his eyes. It could have just been the reflection of the flames. For some reason he couldn't quite pin down, Uncle John sent chills down Brody's spine. Made him feel like a child, scared and alone. And in that moment, Uncle John looked exactly like a monster he could imagine hiding in the closet or under his bed.

Once Brody was able to look away from those burning eyes, he noticed everyone else was staring at him like he was an absolute psycho. Rich wouldn't raise his head and crouched over. It was only when Bart stood up that the everyone looked away from Brody.

"Okay, everyone. Go back to your cabins," he said.

The group disbanded and nobody dared speak. Something had happened, though Brody couldn't figure out what. Uncle John remained stood with his arms behind his back as the campers walked past him. Rich practically stormed away and ran once he got past Uncle John, leaving dust clouds in his trail. The look on his face told Brody he was terrified of the man.

Brody got up from the log while Bart waited with his arms crossed. "I suppose you're expecting me to apologize?" he said to both Bart and Uncle John.

"You broke a very serious rule, young man," Uncle John said. "There are consequences for that."

Brody shook his head. "And what rule was that, exactly? Telling the truth?"

Uncle John continued. "Nobody needs to know why you're here, or what you did to get here. This is a program designed to reform people like yourself. I do not want you to corrupt everyone else's progress."

There was a bite in his tone, but the old man managed to speak in a calm and collected way. His emotionless droll only made him creepier. Brody tried to read Bart's face—was it disappointment, anger or fear? Whatever it was, he stood there anxiously anticipating what was going to be said next.

Eventually Brody admitted defeat. There was no point in being a smart-ass. "Look, I'm sorry, okay?" he began. "You have to understand that it's my second day and I'm still adjusting."

Uncle John placed a large hand on Brody's shoulder. His touch made Brody's stomach lurch. "I understand, perhaps I can overlook this mishap on the basis that it doesn't happen again."

Brody nodded. "No problem."

"I'll take Brody back to his cabin," Bart said, stepping forward. "Goodnight, Uncle John."

"Goodnight, boys," he responded as Bart ushered Brody past him. "And Brody?"

"Yes?"

Uncle John smiled. "No more tales about Silver Oaks or Camp Stanleyside. Okay?"

Before Brody could protest, Bart prodded him forward.

"Okay! I'm going!" he whispered. Brody didn't need to be escorted to his cabin just to hear another of Bart's prep talks. However, Bart grabbed him by the arm, and they walked away from the campfire. Brody turned back to face Uncle John.

He watched him and Bart walk toward the path.

Even at some distance, Brody could swear Uncle John's eyes were still glowing.

CHAPTER V

THE CONCH

Surprisingly, Bart wasn't mad after Brody's outburst. He loosened his arm as soon as they were out of Uncle John's eyesight. His face was dripping with sweat from the heat by the time they got to Cabin 12.

"Bart, what's wrong?" Brody asked.

He fought to catch his breath. Wiped away some sweat plastering hair to his forehead like spikes. "Nothing, I'm just hot, that's all."

"Okay. Look, I'm sorry about before. I—"

Bart smiled and put his hand up. "Like Uncle John said, it was just a small mishap. Just don't do it again. I'm gonna go and lock up for the night. I'll see you in the morning."

Bart rubbed Brody's upper arm and spun on his heels before he could say goodnight.

After Bart had gone, Brody went inside the cabin and was met with four angry faces. Rich was sat on the bed, panting with his head between his legs while Luke kneeled next to him, rubbing his back for support.

Brody moved toward Rich, confused by what was going on. He didn't even have a chance to ask. Luke leaped up from Rich's side and marched over to Brody. He got so close to his face that Brody could feel the heat coming off it.

"I warned you *not* to talk about why you're here,' he said through gritted teeth, "and what do you go and do? Tell the whole camp!"

Unfazed by Luke's aggression, Brody attempted to barge past him so he could get to Rich, who was now being tended to by Akeeb. But with one swift push, Luke blocked him from going anywhere near him.

"What is your fucking problem?" Brody said. "You weren't even there, so why don't you mind your business?"

Josh piped up behind Luke, folding his arms like he was suddenly his bodyguard or something. "It's your fault that Rich is freaking out. Why couldn't you keep your mouth shut and follow the rules?"

Feeling like his head was about to explode, Brody walked in a circle, sighing up at the ceiling. "I swear, if I hear about these *stupid* rules one more time…"

Akeeb stood up to offer his piece. "They're put in place for a reason, Brody. Some of us want to forget about our past and just move on. That's why we're here."

Brody couldn't help but laugh. "You all act like this is some rehabilitation center when it is nothing more than a *fucking prison*! Playing softball in the sun and having stupid campfires at night doesn't change that. You're all delusional."

Among all the arguing, Rich started to pant heavily, but the others were too fired up to pay attention to him. Brody tried for a second time to help him, but Luke remained in between them like a prison guard. Access denied.

"We understand that Brody," Akeeb said. "But those rules are for everyone's safety—including yours."

"*Safety*?" It sounded so ridiculous, but Brody could see the other boys agreed by the look they shared. "What exactly is going on here?"

Luke unfolded his arms and finally broke the barrier

between himself and Rich. Brody waited for an answer, but they all gathered around Rich to calm him down. Luke managed to get Rich to look up and his breathing started to slow.

"I think we've had enough excitement for one day," Luke said with his back turned to Brody. "Why don't we all just get an early night and forget about this?"

Akeeb, Pete and Josh quietly did as they were told. Josh scowled at Brody one last time on his way to bed. Luke sat with Rich while the others turned their lamps off. Brody eyed Luke on the way to his own bed but he ignored him. Perhaps Luke was right, there was enough excitement for one day.

Long after everyone else had gotten to sleep, Brody stared at the ceiling wondering what it was they were all so afraid of.

*

Morning came and everyone in the cabin was silent. Nobody uttered a word as they made their beds, all except for Brody who maybe got an hour—two hours—sleep tops. He grabbed a towel and some fresh clothes, hoping that a shower would help him to wake up.

"Where are you going?" Luke's voice stopped him.

Brody squinted at him and nodded his head toward the towel folded over his arm. "To take a shit and a shower, if that's not against the rules?"

Akeeb rolled his eyes and looked over at Pete. Brody knew they were sick of the animosity between himself and Luke. Brody was too.

"You haven't made your bed. I told you that your bed needs to be made as soon as you're up. We all do, or there's consequences." Luke placed his hands on his hips and took a step toward Brody.

Seeing this as threat, Brody stepped up to him and tip-toed so he could reach his height as much as possible. He didn't find the golden boy intimidating and it was about time Luke learned that.

"If you really want to have a dick-measuring contest then come on, let's fucking go!" Brody's face was an inch away from Luke's. "But I guarantee you I will win."

Just like the night before, Josh was behind Luke with his arms folded, daring Brody to do something. Josh was no threat, though, just a goon that liked to stay on the side-lines.

"Just make the damn bed, Brody," Luke replied, not backing down.

Brody flashed his teeth in a wide grin. "Make it your fucking self, *pretty boy*." He pouted a kiss with his lips.

He came off his tiptoes, intent on walking out of there, but his heels didn't touch the floor. Luke grabbed him in a headlock and tackled Brody to the wooden ground. They rolled around trying to gain control of the fight. Brody felt Luke's weight on top of him, squeezing him against the floor. He kneed at Luke's balls and watched him buckle and recoil. Now that he had the upper hand, Brody climbed on top of him and pinned Luke to the ground with a victorious "Ha!" He raised his fist, ready to smack him right in the mouth. But Akeeb and Pete came from behind, grabbed his arms and pulled him back.

Josh stood by, bouncing up and down like a WWE Superstar. *Wimp.*

Rich was hyperventilating on his bed. He started shaking his head and ran toward the door. "Brody, just do as Luke says. *Please*!" he said, before leaving the cabin.

Without even trying, Brody managed to shake himself free

95

from Akeeb and Pete's grip. He was out of breath, as was Luke who sat on the floor with eyes of fury. There was no point starting a war over an unmade bed, of all the things in the world. Brody offered his hand to Luke so he could get up. Luke pushed it away and got to his feet alone.

The boys waited for their leader to say something. Once he finally got his breath back, he glared at all three and said, "Get out." Brody heard his voice catch in his throat and smiled.

The boys did as they were told, but Luke waited until they were out of the cabin before he spoke. Brody didn't know what to anticipate from the way he looked—another tackle? Maybe even a weapon this time?

No, Luke's too perfect to fight dirty.

"Sit down," Luke said, gesturing to the bed behind Brody. "I'm going to say this to you once, so I need you to listen."

"I'm all ears," Brody said, taking the seat at the end of the bed he was offered.

Luke remained standing before he spoke. "I don't want you—or anyone here—to fuck up all the hard work most of us have put in to becoming better people. If you carry on the way that you are, you'll be gone." He paused. "Just like Jessica."

"Is that a threat?"

"Take it however you want," Luke said, pacing the room now. It reminded Brody of the all the times he was in the principal's office. "But just understand that when people don't adapt here, they go somewhere far worse."

"Oh yeah, and where's that?"

Luke went to say something but hesitated and thought about his next words. "You'll find out," he said, his body starting to quiver, "if you don't change your ways…"

Without another word, Luke left the cabin.

Brody sat down on his bed. Underneath the pillow, he picked up the notebook and looked it over, ready to read on. But he shook his head. Why did he care about some girl's dumb diary? It had caused him enough trouble. He stood up and shoved it into his drawer.

Brody made his bed, just like he was told to.

*

Brody kept his head down for the next few days. He still didn't understand Camp Silver Oaks or the campers, but he'd started to get used to the place. To the fresh air and the activities that, if he were honest, weren't all that stupid as he first thought.

He tried to avoid Luke where he could and began spending most of his time with Daphne. She even managed to sneak him some paper and a pencil so he could draw his own stuff away from Pamela's art class. Of all the things that could be contraband, he still found it hilarious that paper, pencils, or pens fell into that category. During art, they sat watching the campers play archery so Daphne could draw Cynthia, while he did sketches of cartoon characters he'd memorized. More and more versions of Bart Simpson particularly.

During meals, Brody invited Daphne to sit with him, so he didn't have to tolerate Luke. Not that Luke said much to him anyway, which pissed him off even more. It wasn't just Luke's moody silence he couldn't put up with anymore, but also with Pete's chatterbox mouth—the dude never knew when to shut up. The most painful thing about having to endure Pete's stories was that he was like a broken record and kept repeating them. Brody figured that maybe someone laughed about the time he accidently mooned his whole class in the ninth grade, and he thought to stick to that story when he wanted people to laugh with him. And they did—the whole table laughed along—even Daphne. The first time and the tenth time.

"Do you seriously find Pete funny?" Brody asked her one night after dinner.

Daphne shrugged. "He's a dork, but he's a cute dork."

"Cynthia *and* Pete, huh?" Brody laughed. "That's like ketchup and mayonnaise."

"I like my ketchup and mayonnaise mixed together."

"Damn, you have strange tastes."

Daphne grinned and bounced her eyebrows up-and-down. "I know."

For the sake of not starting anymore fights with Luke and keeping out of trouble, Brody reserved his sarcastic nature around his cabin buddies. After the fight, they were cautious around each other. Josh looked like he was ready to throw a punch whenever they locked eyes, not that he expected that Josh could throw a punch. But eventually he softened.

Art class became a bore and as much as Brody enjoyed his conversations with Daphne, he wanted to try something else. While they sat in their usual spot, observing the campers' archery skills, Brody got up and wandered over to Bart.

"Why don't you show me how to use that thing?" he said, nodding at the bow on the ground.

Bart shook his head. "Sorry Brody, you haven't been here long enough to qualify for target practice."

Down the line of targets, Brody saw Luke watching them. He raised a curious eyebrow at Brody before turning his attention back to the target and firing a bow right in the center—bullseye. Luke walked over to the target and pulled the bow out with one swift tug.

Such a showoff.

"What do I have to do to qualify?" Brody asked, turning his back from Luke.

Bart scratched his head. "Well, you need to have been here for more than six months and be on your best behavior for starters."

"Well, I can't promise that."

Bart smiled, showing off his crystal-white teeth. Cocked his head in an oddly flirtatious way. "Yeah, I suspected as much. Why don't you try basketball or canoeing? Of course, it would mean that you would need a group and a counselor with you…"

Canoeing. It wasn't a bad idea. Not only would it be a change of scenery, but it would allow him to see the surrounding areas of the camp.

"Okay," Brody said to Bart's surprise. "I'll assemble a team."

Brody walked back over to Daphne and sat next to her. She was concentrating so hard on drawing that she didn't even acknowledge his return.

"Let's go canoeing."

She stopped drawing but didn't raise her head from her sketchbook. "No thanks."

"Come on, don't you want a bit of freedom?"

Daphne gathered her things and stood. Her face gave nothing away, but Brody could see she was either pissed off or upset. When she finally looked at him, he frowned at her, unsure of what he'd done wrong.

"I'll have my freedom soon enough, thanks," she said before storming away.

*

Confused about Daphne's ruffled feathers, Brody returned to

the cabin where Rich, Pete, Akeeb and Josh were all sitting on their beds. Pete was reading a book about different kinds of birds—*boring*—while Josh was refolding his clothes. Akeeb and Rich were talking about Captain Marvel or something but stopped as soon as Brody entered the cabin.

"I have an idea," he said. "Why don't we all go canoeing?"

Silence.

Josh stopped folding his clothes, Pete shot his head up and Akeeb instantly looked away. But it was Rich who seemed to be the most stunned by the suggestion and started to shake.

Brody fidgeted with his hands. He felt like he was butt-naked on stage. "I just thought it would be something fun to do," he said, "y'know, as a group so that we can bond…or whatever."

Brody didn't even convince himself with the lie. He suspected they called bullshit on his reason for wanting to do something so out of the ordinary for him, too. He waited patiently for an answer, but he got nothing. And then suddenly, Rich started hyperventilating—it was like he had been told someone had just died.

"Rich?" Brody asked.

The other boys rushed to Rich as he clutched at his chest, his face the color of beetroot with streaks of fresh sweat and tears riding down his face. Brody stood back with his mouth wide open, trying to understand the reaction. It wasn't until he was pushed aside that he even noticed Luke had come into the cabin.

"What's happened?" Luke asked no one in particular, crouching down at eye-level with Rich. "Rich—Rich, look at me!" He pointed two fingers underneath his eyes.

Akeeb rubbed Rich's back. "Brody suggested that we go

canoeing in the lake together and—"

"Rich!" Luke said once more, cutting Akeeb off. "Look at me and breath—just breath. You don't have to go in the lake, okay? It was just a suggestion."

Despite Luke's calming technique, Rich continued to panic, shaking his head, and gritting his teeth together. "The eyes," he said, breathlessly, "the eyes…"

"I—I'm sorry," Brody said, holding his hands up. "I didn't mean to upset him."

Luke turned to Brody, frowning at first but then his face softened. "It's fine, Brody," he said, "Rich just has a fear of water, that's all. You weren't to know."

It made sense now. Brody knelt next to Luke and placed his hand on Rich's shaking arm. "I'm really sorry. I didn't realize it was a trigger."

Slowly, Rich's breathing returned to normal. He kept his eyes ahead and nodded along with Luke until the red in his face disappeared. "Thanks guys, I don't know what came over me."

"It's fine," Luke said, standing up. "It's getting late in the day anyway. Brody, why don't you take us to the arts building and show us how to draw or something?"

The request came at a surprise, but Brody saw it for what it was: an olive branch. Luke wanted to start getting along, even if it was for the sake of keeping Rich calm.

"I'd love to," he said, smiling at Luke, genuinely.

While Brody led the way out of the cabin, his mind switched back to the lake. He thought about the large *thing* he saw on his first night and wondered if Rich had seen it, too. Was that why he became so frantic? Then the entry about the raft in the notebook. Brody hadn't even looked at it since the night of the campfire.

The eyes.

Rich mentioned something about eyes. Maybe that's why he was so scared—it wasn't the water itself, but what might be in it.

*

After showing the boys how to draw simple things like trees, flowers, and fruit, they went back to the cabin to freshen up before dinner. Brody and Luke both went to the shower block at the same time. They walked together in silence and took the spare cubicles at the end of the row. The other campers started to clear out one by one and eventually it was just Brody and Luke left.

"Thank you," Luke said over the dribbling water.

Brody shook the water out of his face and leaned over the cubicle barrier. "For what?"

"For trying."

"I just wanted to see the lake if, I'm being honest."

Luke turned off the shower and leaned back against the barrier. His naked body in full view. "I know, but you still made the effort to include yourself into the group. It's good for you."

"Do I get a gold star or something?"

"No, but you might start earning some respect from the higher-ups. Believe me, in this place, that's exactly what you want."

Higher-ups? Brody pondered on the thought.

The way Luke said it was as though he was warning him, just not in the way he usually would. He considered asking Luke more about Rich's panic attack, but he knew it would probably lead to another argument or a fight. For the first time, Brody really studied Luke's face and noticed that he had some heavy stubble coming through. He looked older than he was, like he'd been carrying a heavy burden for far too long.

"How much longer are you here for, if you don't mind me asking?"

"I do mind," Luke said, snapping the plastic curtain back and wandering to the sink to grab his towel. He placed it around his waist and ran his fingers through his wet hair. "Don't spoil it for yourself, Brody," he continued, staring at him through the foggy mirror. "Just accept that you're here for as long as you are."

Luke threw his clothes on and wiped at the mirror. Brody came out of the cubicle and stood next to him, looking at his blood-shot eyes from the water. "It's hard for me to understand this place. I should be in a jail—a real jail. I don't understand why I was sent here or why *anyone* was sent here. You've got to admit that you thought the same thing when they sentenced you."

"I just assumed I was one of the lucky ones," Luke said, avoiding Brody's eyes. "An experimental rehabilitation center where I don't have the fear of getting shivved at every corner I turn—most people who do wrong don't get that luxury. We should all be grateful."

"But that's the thing, Luke. There is no rehabilitation. We're just expected to adjust to this place and reform. It doesn't make any sense to me."

Luke sighed. "It will."

Brody watched Luke leave the showers. Of course, he wanted Luke to elaborate, but he knew better than to push him.

It will...

*

Rich didn't come to dinner. Brody and the boys left him to get some rest as he was tired, and Luke agreed to sneak some food back to the cabin for him. Brody was surprised that Luke would break one of the rules but admired him for being a decent friend. On the way to the mess hall, he heard Josh complaining to Akeeb.

"Sure, because Luke says it's fine, we all just go along with it…" he said, trying to be discreet. "If that was anyone else, he would have dragged us to the mess hall."

"Josh," Akeeb hissed, "shut up."

For once, Josh did shut up and sulked through the whole of dinner. Daphne didn't sit with Brody and his cabin buddies, even though he signaled for her to come over. She just turned away and made conversation with a girl in her own cabin. It seemed Pete was confused by her absence too and kept looking over at her.

"Have I done something to upset Daphne?" he asked Brody.

Akeeb answered for him. "Maybe she's just bored to death of hearing your stories."

"Hey! I thought you liked my stories!"

"We did," Luke said, "the first few times."

Akeeb started to laugh and everyone besides Josh joined in—even Pete. In the corner of his eye, Brody spotted Uncle John at the counselor's table, staring at them. He tried to avoid directly looking at him, but it was hard to pretend. Whatever his reason was for staring, it made Brody shiver. He could practically feel his eyes burning into him.

The eyes.

The spell was broken when Bart approached the table. "Hey guys, no Rich tonight?"

"He wasn't feeling too good," Luke answered. "I let Pamela know on the way in."

"Nothing too serious I hope? Does he need me to look him over in the infirmary?"

"Just some stomach cramps," Brody said. "I'm sure he'll be fine after a good night's rest."

Bart nodded and looked down at Brody's plate. "Brody, I was wondering, do you want to go for a walk with me when you're done?"

The other boys looked from Bart to Brody. Luke even cocked an eyebrow at him, which made Brody's face redden.

"Just to discuss how you're getting on with everything," Bart continued. "If you don't have any other plans after dinner, that is."

"He's free," Luke said, turning the corner of his mouth slightly.

Before things could get more awkward, Brody stood up and grabbed his plate. "I'm free now. Let's go."

After dropping his plate by the cleaning station and waving at the cook, they walked out of the mess hall. On the way past, Brody noticed that Uncle John still had his eyes fixed on him. He shivered one more time once they were out in the open air.

The evening was cool and crisp, and the camp seemed still. The sky was just turning over into night and the last hues of flamingo pink were fading away to make room for the stars. Once they were away from the noise in the mess hall, Brody looked up and smiled. It was a beautiful night.

"Was that a genuine moment of happiness I just witnessed, Brody Jackson?" Bart teased. "You're changing your tune."

Brody's face reddened once again. "Well, it is exhausting being cynical every waking moment of your life—it's an art, in fact. But I suppose I can let my guard down around you."

"I'm glad you've made some friends, even Luke, if I'm not mistaken."

"Hmm, he's not bad," Brody said with a shrug. "I still think he's a kiss-ass, but I can live with that."

Bart rolled his eyes. "Well, I'm glad you've given him a fair chance. He's a good guy."

"Yeah, I guess he is."

They carried on down the trail toward the cabins, until they found a spot by an old oak tree. They had a great view of the bend in the lake from there. Bart started to shiver. The temperature had dropped, and he was only dressed in a camp regulation top—that he had cropped himself—and high-waisted shorts. Retro tunes and retro fashion sense. Even though it wouldn't fit him, Brody took off his hoodie and passed it to Bart.

"Here," he said.

While Brody held the hoodie out to him, Bart eyed it cautiously. He opened his mouth to speak and stopped himself. He sighed and started again. "Brody, I just want you to know that I think you're a great guy, but—"

Even without letting him finish, Brody knew what he was getting at. "Don't read too much into it, dude. I'm just offering my hoodie. Not the key to my chastity belt. It's cold and I'm warm, so please just take it."

Bart nodded. Even though it was tight around his arms and wouldn't go all the way around his thick torso to zip up, he still wore it and smiled. Brody smiled back and held his gaze when he took a step toward him. Bart shivered, this time from nerves, as Brody placed a hand on his waist and moved closer into his body. Hot breaths blew onto Brody's cheeks, their faces only inches apart.

"Do you want me to stop?" Brody asked.

Bart shook his head and placed his giant hand on the back of Brody's head, guiding him in. Before their mouths could touch, they were interrupted by a buzzing sound that traveled through the camp. It sounded like some sort of horn, but not the one they used in the mornings.

"What's that?" Brody said, looking around as some campers emerged from the mess hall. Bart took a step away from Brody, his face dropped, and he stared at the ground. The other campers had dread written all over their faces.

Bart closed his eyes and bit his lip before he finally answered. "It's the conch."

Brody knew what a conch was, but he still didn't understand what it meant. He shook his head as the other campers marched up the trail past the mess hall.

"Come on," Bart said. "Follow me."

When Bart began to walk away, Brody grabbed his arm. "Wait! What is it? Why is everyone rushing?"

Tears pooled in Bart's eyes, making them glassy like he was a porcelain doll. The way he looked at Brody also made him appear just as fragile. All his confidence had been drained. He didn't answer Brody. Instead, he shook his arm away and followed the crowd.

Bart stormed ahead, weaving around the campers to get in front of them. Brody tried to catch up, running after him. Near the mess hall, Luke came running out with Josh, Akeeb and Pete behind him.

"Guys, what's going on?" Brody asked.

None of them said anything. Just exchanged secretive glances.

Brody raced up the steps. "Please, for fucks sake, can we stop with all the secrets and just tell me?"

Luke barged past Brody, making him stumble. Akeeb and Pete couldn't meet his eyes, but Josh smiled at him like everything was fine.

They boys joined the other campers and made their way down the path. The one that lead to—

The lake...

The campers were all heading toward the lake.

CHAPTER VI

THE LAKE

Brody was the last one to make it down to the lake. The campers had gathered on the mound before the dock. On both sides of the dock were two pillar torches. Orange flames flickered in the heavy breeze. Some of the counselors, including Bart, stood at the foot of the dock. He had his hands folded and wouldn't look up from the ground. Uncle John stood next to him, looking directly at Brody as he made his way into the silent crowd. Once he had finally found a place to settle, Uncle John turned around and climbed to the top step of the dock.

Hushed whispers, concerned faces and frantic pointing at Uncle John, waiting for him to speak. He opened his arms out to the campers and lost the calm expression on his face.

"We provide an excellent environment here at Camp Silver Oaks. All of you are lucky to be here. All of you are lucky to have escaped a much worse fate. And yet..." he paused, looking around at his prisoners. "...yet, some of you show your gratitude by deceiving me!"

Blood rushed to Uncle John's face. A thick vein popped from his neck. Gone was the enthusiastic leader encouraging everyone to bask in the joy of the day. What stood before them was a man striking them down like a powerful god, ready to cast the ultimate judgment.

"Hear, hear!" Luke chanted to Brody's left, raising his fist in the air.

Brody looked around the crowd of campers. They followed his lead, repeating Luke's sentiment, including Daphne who briefly locked eyes with Brody before turning away. Bart also joined in, reluctantly it seemed.

Uncle John waited for the crowd's silence before continuing. "One of your fellow campers has let us down—let *you* down! He has shamed all of us with his deceit."

He.

Brody scanned the crowd. He couldn't believe he'd forgotten about him. Rich. He wasn't there. Hadn't come out from the cabin with everyone else. Brody's heart sank.

"He tried to leave!" Uncle John yelled. "He tried to run away from the little corner of paradise that we created for you. So you can redeem yourselves from the *disgusting* human beings that you used to be before coming here."

Brody felt the blood boiling below his skin, burning to push out of every pore. He wanted to run from the crowd and punch Uncle John right in the jaw. Knock some sense into the old man. His false demeanor shined through, and so did the demeanor of Camp Silver Oaks. It wasn't a reform facility, it wasn't even a prison. It was a cult, and everyone had been sucked in by his venomous philosophy.

The man was a monster.

Uncle John nodded down at Bart and Pamela. They walked away briefly, as all heads turned in their direction. When they came back, they held Rich by his biceps, a gag stuffed in his mouth. He tried to scream and cry, but his voice was muffled through the rag.

There was pure terror in his face. Nobody did anything. Nobody questioned. Nobody said anything. Just waited with bated breath for whatever was coming next. The more that Rich struggled, Bart gritted his teeth. He looked as though he was ready to swipe Rich hard across the face to make him stop. Brody's feet were ready to fly off the ground until Luke's hand appeared on his shoulder.

"We *can't* do anything, or it will be us next," he whispered into Brody's ear, gripping him by the arms. "*Don't. Fucking. Move.*"

Brody shook his head, fought against Luke's grip, but he was too strong. "I'm not gonna stand here and do nothing," he said. "They're hurting him!"

With all the strength he had, Brody tried once again to wiggle out of Luke's hold. He wanted to march right up to Uncle John, whose attention he managed to gain. Uncle John's empty expression fired Brody up even more.

Bart glanced over, noticing the commotion. Brody hoped his pleading eyes would make him come to his senses, but he just hardened his face and yanked Rich to keep him still.

How could he participate in this? Was it all just an act? Being Mr. Nice Guy. Was everything an act?

Rich clocked eyes with Brody, choking himself with tears behind the gag, screaming out to him.

"Richard," Uncle John began, forcing Rich to look up at him. "You have broken your promise to become a better citizen of society. You have betrayed all of us and for that you must face the consequences. You've spoiled your chances, and now you must walk the dock."

"Hear, hear!" Luke bellowed behind Brody. Everyone joined in, raising closed fists to the sky. Some smiling, others close to tears. He spotted Cynthia quickly push one away from her eye.

)))

Rich struggled and screamed as loud as he could. Bart and Pamela dragged him up the dock. Brody tried to elbow Luke in the ribs, but Luke wrapped his arms around Brody's arms and stomach.

"You can't save him," he said, emotionless. "None of us can."

Halfway down the dock, Bart removed Rich's gag. He pushed the guy so hard that he fell forward, sliding near the end of the wooden plank. His screams had become heavy sobs, between hyperventilations. He looked back at them all—a blubbering mess.

Bart and Pamela stood back as Rich cowered at the end of the dock and looked out at the black water. Patiently, Uncle John stood with his back to the campers, resting his hands in front of him.

Brody convinced himself that they were going to push him into the lake. Didn't see the significance at first.

And then he remembered. *His biggest fear is water. Not just water, but the lake.*

That thing. The creature.

The eyes.

The *thing* he saw on his first day, the way Pamela wouldn't let him go anywhere near the lake. The way Bart treated him when he caught him there alone. Rich's panic attack. The entry in the notebook about *something* hitting the raft.

"Luke," Brody said, "what the *fuck* is in that lake?"

He didn't respond, just tightened his arms around Brody. Squeezed so hard he thought he was going to puke.

And then the sound came. Like thunder. Just like Brody heard the first night in the cabin. It deafened the crowd. Some of the campers looked away, like it hit them square in the face.

Others watched on with wide eyes, waiting. A few raised their hands to the sky, praying to it like a deity. When the thunder stopped, the air was silent. Not a gasp or a breath could be heard among the crowd.

Then it erupted from the lake. Erect and towering high above Rich like a skyscraper.

Brody's eyes expanded. Every fear he had flashed before him and hit him like a cluster of heavy rocks. Every nightmare absorbed him. He followed its slim, black, scaled body, shining like glitter from the salty residue of the lake. He followed it all the way to its head.

"*Jesus Christ.*"

Blood-red eyes reflected in the moonlight with a menacing, hypnotic gaze as it stretched out its jaw into a wide yawn. It hissed—a loud hiss—dropping a forked tongue from the fleshy pink of its mouth, revealing two gigantic sharp fangs. As Rich's screams echoed throughout the camp, the monstrous serpent's head expanded into a diamond-shaped hood. The snake crashed down on Rich, impaling him with its fangs.

Brody shot his head away. His mouth trembled and the rest of his body went numb. He wanted to scream, but nothing would come out even if he tried. Everyone watched on—some in disgust, some terrified, others without an ounce of remorse. The serpent slid its giant head off the dock, deflating its hood and disappeared back below the surface, dragging Rich's mangled body with it.

Uncle John turned to the campers. "The judgment has been cast," he said, grinning.

"Hear, hear!" Everyone chanted.

"Let this remind us that life is fleeting," Uncle John bellowed. "That we only get *this* life. Let this remind us to make the most of it."

Uncle John's eyes were kind now, as though he wanted the lesson to be heard by all. As though he didn't want this to happen to anyone else.

Brody wasn't convinced.

The campers stated to scatter away and walk back to the camp.

Brody wiped away the tears that ran down his cheeks, swallowed down the sour saliva rolling around in his mouth. Luke eased his grip on him and gently released his arms from around Brody's waist. For a few seconds he lingered behind, before trailing back to camp with the others. Daphne stared straight through him like he was a stranger.

When Brody braved looking over at the dock, Uncle John stood there, staring down at him like a regal king. No pity. He bowed his head at Brody like he had just committed a good deed. Between heavy breaths and blurry tears, Brody looked away as Uncle John stepped down from the dock. On his way past, he tapped Brody on the shoulder. His touch felt like being stabbed in the gut several times over.

The last two people at the dock were Brody and Bart. Bart approached him slowly, but Brody couldn't even look at him. He turned his face and didn't hide the heavy sobs that followed. Of course, he wanted to go ballistic, ask him why—and how— he could do what he'd just done. But all Brody could manage in that moment was shock.

Bart opened his mouth, licked his bottom lip.

"I'm sorry," he finally managed, before walking past Brody and leaving him alone to watch the ripples settle on the water.

Ten minutes later, Brody walked back into the camp. Noise came from the mess hall. He couldn't understand how they could all act like nothing had just happened.

When he got back to his cabin, nobody else was inside, which he was grateful for. He didn't know how he would react if he saw any of his cabin buddies—especially Luke. Brody looked over at Rich's bed. Perfectly made, just like the rules stated. But now it would be empty—permanently empty of Rich—and a haunting reminder.

On the bottom of his own bed, Brody noticed that the hoodie he gave to Bart had been returned. Neatly folded. He sat on the bed and held the hoodie in his hands, smelling Bart's scent all over it. He buried his face into it, sobbing once again before he clenched both his hands into the material and attempted to rip it apart. The teeth of the zip dug into his skin and the jersey burned his hands from the friction. Eventually he gave up and threw it on the floor.

Brody sobbed into his hands. "Mom, *Mommy.*"

After a moment, he took his face out of his hands and looked at the knob on his bedside drawer. He pulled it open and grabbed the notebook, looking at it for the first time in days.

Last night, something really bad happened. Something <u>TERRIBLE.</u>

Some of the campers had a baseball game going in the afternoon and I'd never been very good at it, so I just watched while some of the counselors joined in. I noticed Marla and some of the other girls looking at me and laughing. I ignored it at first, but they just made it so obvious the more they carried on. I walked over to them, and Marla put her finger to her mouth. They stopped.

"What's so funny, Marla?" I asked. "Is there something you want to say to me?"

Marla stood up straight with her hands behind her back. "Yeah, *nice tits.*"

"Excuse me?"

The girls burst into fits of laughter. Marla kept her hands behind her back.

"Okay, hand it over," I said.

"Hand *what* over?"

I put my hand out, but Marla just raised an eyebrow at it. I was done with taking shit off this kid. I was done being a pushover. So, I grabbed her wrist.

"*Ow!* You're hurting me!" Marla screamed, commanding the attention of everybody around.

I didn't give a damn if she caused a scene. Once I managed to pull her hand forward, I swiped the photo she was holding onto. A photo of me. The one Tina took when I came running out the shower.

"Where did you get this?" I tightened my grip on her wrist.

Marla started to fake-cry. "I found it! Let go you fucking psycho!"

"Found it *where?*"

Before she could answer, Rusty came running behind her and pulled Marla out of my grip. "Jesus!" he said. "What the hell are you doing?"

Marla, dramatic as always, leaned into Rusty and wrapped her arms around him. She pretended to sob.

"It's alright, Marla." Rusty put his hand on her head and turned his attention back to me. "What's wrong with you? You really hurt her!"

The way Rusty yelled made my adrenaline rush. I hated the way he looked at me, like I really was a fucking psycho. But then I looked down at the photo in my hand, and I didn't care what he thought of me in that moment. I was angry. I scrunched the photo in my fist and put it into my pocket.

Rusty looked down at my hand and his face softened. I'm not sure if he saw what it was. "What's going on?"

"Ask your girlfriend," I said, before I turned and walked away.

I went to Tina's cabin straight after. She was outside with Nancy and Lydia laying on towels in their bathing suits. I marched over, fished the photo out of my pocket and threw it at her.

"What the fuck!" she said, sitting up and removing her shades. "What do *you* want?"

"Do your worst, Tina," I said, shaking. "Show it to everyone for all I care. I'm done with your shit!"

Tina opened the crumpled photo and started laughing. "Oh yeah, that. How did that get out?"

She glanced over at Nancy and Lydia who covered their smirks.

"I did as you said. I kept away from Rusty, and I kept out of your way. Why do you have to be such a bitch?"

Tina stood up, towering over me like the blonde amazon she was. "You really think I give a damn about Rusty? You think that's what this is about? He's just a summer fling, darlin'. Someone to play with while I'm here. I could do so much better than some hick."

"Is that right?" a voice said behind Tina. I looked past her to see Rusty standing there with his hands in his pockets.

Tina's face dropped. She quickly spun round. "Rusty, I—"

"No, you know what?" he said. "She's right, you are a bitch."

Rusty marched past us, down the path back to the main part of camp. Tina pushed past me and ran after him.

"Rusty! I didn't mean it! Wait!"

Nancy and Lydia didn't know where to look.

Tina and Rusty didn't come to dinner. Nancy and Lydia looked lost without their leader and ate their dinner without saying anything, occasionally looking over at me. Lydia even offered me a smile which I didn't return. I sat next to Andy who nodded over at the empty chairs.

"Trouble in paradise?" he asked.

"Something like that."

"How terrible." Andy grinned.

I got up to leave, ready to walk back to my cabin when I felt a tap on my shoulder. It was Andy.

"Wanna hang out tonight?" he asked.

I was surprised by the abrupt offer. I was even a little hesitant. But I nodded. "That would be nice."

It was getting dark by the time we stepped outside. The nights were drawing in sooner each day. Andy and I headed down the path toward the lake, which I hadn't been to since the raft turned over. It was so peaceful with nobody else about.

"So, I heard about today," Andy said after a while. "It was pretty bad-ass."

"*Bad-ass*?" I said, "Me? You must have the wrong girl."

"No, I'm definitely talking about you. I like most of the kids, but Marla? She's a little brat. I'm glad you stood up to her."

I nodded. "Thanks. But her parents are probably going to get me fired when they find out. So, there's that. You know what, though? It was worth it."

"Well, I'll have your back," Andy said.

Andy didn't know the full story and he didn't need to know. It was a genuine statement and it felt good to finally have a friend here.

We walked just past the lake when Andy stopped. "Do you want to go in the woods?"

"Won't we get lost? It's getting pretty dark." I didn't like the idea of not being able to see where we were going.

"It's okay, I know the trails pretty well."

I agreed and we stepped into the woods. The further we went in, the darker it got. Surprisingly, it didn't bother me so much. I felt safe with

Andy. We talked about school, where we wanted to go to college, and I found out that The Sisters of Mercy wasn't a catholic school.

"Are you ready to head back?" he said.

I didn't even know how long we'd been in there. "Yeah, it's probably getting late."

We made our way back through the same trails we walked, but both of us stopped when we heard something snap. I looked at Andy and he shrugged, but then we heard it again. This was followed by the sounds of leaves crunching, and *someone* panting.

That someone was running right toward us.

My first reaction was to scream. Andy picked up the nearest stick he could find, ready to swing it behind his shoulders and attack them.

"Wait-wait-wait!" they said. "It's me! It's Rusty!"

Rusty was out of breath, I couldn't really see him, but the flashes of moonlight showed that he was covered in something shiny. And red. Blood.

I took a step back and grabbed onto Andy's arm. "Rusty, what happened to you?"

"She's dead!"

"Who?"

"Tina!"

I couldn't believe what I was hearing. I looked over at Andy, unable to read his face in the dark.

"How?" Andy asked.

Rusty just uttered, "A snake."

REST OF ENTRY TORN OUT

*

The next day, Brody walked into the mess hall. Everyone stopped. The sound of Brody's footsteps toward the serving window filled the room as he helped himself to some sausage, bacon, scrambled eggs, and a glass of orange juice. The cook avoided his gaze, but what he could see of her face looked miserable. Was she on board with the snake stuff like everyone else?

On the way to a bench, Uncle John waited patiently to see what he would do. Or say. They all stared.

"It's a beautiful day, isn't it?" Brody said, smiling brightly around the room.

When he sat down, the laughter and joy resumed, echoing throughout the mess hall.

Across the room, Brody spotted Bart looking at him—glum and guilty. Brody raised his glass and drank his orange juice.

Just wait, Brody, he thought.

You're getting out of here.

.

EPILOGUE

Pete looked behind him, making sure nobody saw him or followed him down the path. Most of the campers were in the mess hall playing board games, and he could hear some dumb music coming from Bart's cabin. That Tears for Fears song he was always playing around the campfire—*Head Over Heels.* He'd been listening to that a lot recently.

It was just after 9:00pm now. She would be in the woods, waiting for him:

MEET ME IN THE WOODS AFTER 9.

I NEED TO TALK TO YOU. ALONE.

D

Pete was surprised to see the note on his pillow after dinner. Daphne had ignored him for a few days now. She ignored everyone. And to leave it out in the open? He knew it was against the rules to go out to the woods alone, and he was scared someone might see him. After what happened to Rich, the boys in Cabin 12 were on pins and needles—except for Josh and Brody. It was like somebody had done a lobotomy on Brody. He was so cheerful and chirpy all the time. It was actually getting kind of annoying. Luke was miserable, as always. But the difference was, he'd barely said a word to him or the others since Rich's—*what would you even call it?*—punishment.

Akeeb was his closest friend, but he was spending a lot of

time alone. There was a darkness in his eyes that Pete had never seen before. Akeeb had completely shut down.

"Talk to me, dude," Pete said, only yesterday. He found Akeeb sitting alone, resting his back against a tree near the main field. His eyes fixed firmly on the lake. "What's done is done."

Akeeb bit his lip. "You know, when I was a kid, I always imagined monsters like that. I was always scared of snakes. My dad told me I was childish, even teased me with his buddy's python after one too many sometimes. Arabelle. That was the snake's name."

Pete sat down next to him. "I…I didn't know that." And why would he? Akeeb had barely mentioned his family before. "I'm sorry."

"I had a pet hamster once." Akeeb smiled. "He was called Thor, named after my favorite superhero, obviously."

"I wouldn't expect anything less from a nerd like you." Pete knocked his shoulder into Akeeb, hoping that teasing him would make him laugh. It didn't, he just stared ahead.

"One night my dad and his buddy were drinking after a game, not that he ever needed an excuse." Tears pooled in Akeeb's eyes. He swallowed a lump in his throat before he continued. "Dad came into my room, woke me up because he was all over the place, and took Thor out of his cage and stumbled over to the kitchen. Arabelle was curled up in the plastic box where I kept my action figures. They were on the floor, some of them missing arms and legs.

"My dad held Thor by his tiny tail, just above the box. Said, 'Let's see how super Thor really is now!' before he dropped him in there. I ran over, ready to stick my hand in to rescue him, but my dad shoved me to the ground. Next thing, I hear

Thor squealing and my dad's laugh—I'll never forget it."

"Fuck…" Pete didn't know what else to say. By comparison to what he'd seen since he arrived at Camp Silver Oaks, the death of Akeeb's pet hamster was nothing. But what his dad did to him? "That's terrible."

Akeeb turned to Pete. "What my dad did was evil. He was evil. And what Uncle John did to Rich—and all the others he's fed to that *monster*—is evil."

"You know the rules. We just need to stick to them, and we won't end up on that dock."

"Won't we?" Akeeb scoffed. "How many people actually *leave* this place?"

Of course people had left. They did their time and they got to go home. That was the deal. "Yes. I've seen plenty of people get out of here."

Akeeb stood up. "Get real, Pete. Do you really think all those people left and didn't plan to blab about all the deaths? The fact there's a *gigantic* fucking snake living out there? Uncle John expects that. I don't think any of us are ever making it out here. Not alive, at least."

As he watched Akeeb walk away, Pete noticed Pamela in the window of one of the cabins, staring at him. He waved, but she didn't return the gesture.

*

Pete walked past the lake, briefly glancing over at the dock. Scared to look for too long in case he saw…*it*. He couldn't believe Rich was gone or that he'd tried to escape. What was he thinking? He knew that Uncle John had eyes everywhere. And with that thought, Pete began to think that coming out to the woods wasn't a good move either.

Now was his chance. Turn around and go back to camp.

"*Fuck!*" he cussed, before entering the woods.

Pete took the trail for a couple of hundred yards, looking behind him to check he hadn't been followed. He had never been in the woods at night before. He had no idea *where* in the woods he was meant to be meeting Daphne.

"Daph?" he said, cautious that he shouldn't be too loud. "Are you here?"

He heard the occasional rustle of leaves. Small animals scurrying around in the distance. No sign of Daphne—no sign of anybody. Rubbing at his bare arms to keep the bugs away, he walked a little further down the trail. After a moment, Pete called out Daphne's name one last time before giving up.

The bugs started to tickle his neck. *This fucking heat.* Pete went to scratch at it, feeling something thick rest around his collarbone. Knotted and scratchy. "What the—"

Within seconds a rope tightened around his neck. He hovered above the ground, kicking his feet, trying to dig his fingers under the noose. It was no use.

It was getting tighter and tighter.

He kicked harder, struggling at the rope as he was lifted higher into the air. His vision became blurry. Blood rushed to his head. Footsteps approached behind him, crunching the leaves on the ground. Pete's Adam's Apple thrashed inside his throat, begging for air.

The person forward, turning in the thin slither of moonlight that revealed their face.

Pete's eyes widened. "*Pl-ea-se*"

But they just stood there, watching him struggle. Grinning.

Pete's eyelids became heavy. He couldn't keep them open much longer. As his lids closed, he looked into his killer's eyes.

The eyes of someone he trusted.

TO BE CONTINUED...

CAMPER COMMENTS

"Camp Silver Oaks is like going to Sleepaway Camp on Fear Street."

Christopher Robertson - author of The Cotton Candy Massacre.

"Fancy a blend of Friday the 13th and Lovecraftian Horror? Then Leeroy has the story for you."

Jamie Stewart - author of Montague's Carnival of Delights and Terror.

"Cross James does a wonderful job in capturing the retro vibes of the 1980s in the this YA Gay Horror."

David-Jack Fletcher - author of The Haunting of Harry Peck.

ACKNOWLEDGEMENTS

I'd like to start off by thanking my wonderful husband, **Mark**. For his constant support and encouragement with my writing. As well as his questionable ideas for future stories and novels...

Christopher Robertson, thank you for all your help getting this book to publication. Creating the backmatter, reading an early draft of *Silver Oaks* and offering constructive advice for it to reach its full potential. And of course, for providing a quote for the blurb. I'm honoured and eternally grateful to you. **Samuel M. Hallam**, for your excellent feedback in the early stages, too. **Donnie Goodman**, for creating that *killer* cover. **Andrew "The Book Dad" Robert**, for always being there for support and using your resources to help the Horror Community out.

Horror in general. The books, the movies, the TV shows, for keeping me company as a child and shaping me into the crazy fan I am today.

A special thanks to the faculty of **the Creative Writing department at Liverpool John Moores University** for teaching me everything I know. And for pushing me to achieve my best. I hope I've done you all proud.

And finally, to my friend and editor, **David-Jack Fletcher**. I couldn't have finished this book without you. You went above and beyond for me when you didn't have to, reigned me in during my bad days with the book, and pushed me to keep going. There are not enough thank-yous in the world to express how grateful I am for what you have done for me and *Silver Oaks*.

ABOUT THE AUTHOR

Leeroy Cross James is a horror writer from the U.K. His short stories have been featured in several anthologies including *Beach Bodies* from DarkLit Press and *The Omens Call* from Devils Rock Publishing.

He is a self-certified Slasher Horror fanatic with a particular interest in the early 80s boom of the subgenre. Some of his favourite horror films are *Friday the 13th*, *Sleepaway Camp*, *Urban Legend,* and *Prom Night.* Absolute **Slashics**!

He once met Adrienne King (Alice from *Friday the 13th*) and Felissa Rose (Angela from *Sleepaway Camp)* on the same day, hugged them, told them how much those movies meant to him and cried right after doing so.

His dream would be to spend a night at Camp Crystal Lake.

CAMP SILVER OAKS is his first book.

Follow me on social media!

INSTAGRAM: @LEEROYCROSSJAMES

TWITTER: @ZombiLeeroy

Printed in Great Britain
by Amazon

84722027R00079